D1531988

JUST LEFT OF LUCKY

Dianna Dorisi Winget

Just Left of Lucky

Copyright © 2018 by Dianna Dorisi Winget

CHAPTER ONE

T HE WHITE FREIGHTLINER pulled in close enough to shake our Chevy Impala. Aunt Junie jerked her head from the driver's window with a fitful jump, but ten seconds later she was sawing logs again. I didn't understand how anyone could sleep through the racket of a semi-truck idling ten feet away. I prodded her shoulder. "Aunt Junie, wake up."

The little plastic clock taped to the dash read 5:18, and the wonderful, greasy scents wafting over from the deli were driving me crazy. I prodded again. "Aunt Junie, c'mon. Can we please go for dinner?"

We still had Gatorade, potato chips and Cheerios in the plastic bin in the trunk, plus some granola bars and peanut butter. But I craved something hot and not just a snack. I flipped open the glove box. There were two five dollar bills and a bunch of quarters. I nibbled my lip, undecided. The last thing I wanted was to give Aunt Junie another reason to resent me, but tequila always made her sleep longer, and I was afraid I might starve to death by the time she woke up. I grabbed a five and crumpled it in my fist.

Boone witnessed my criminal activity from his perch in the back window, looking spring-loaded as always, his little ears peaked and his tongue sticking out a quarter inch. I winked at him. "You stay here and be a good boy, okay? Be right back."

I shoved open the Impala's heavy door and scrambled out before Boone could follow. The strong scent of diesel burned my nose and reminded me of the stink around old Mrs. Zilinksy's—our neighbor back in Idaho—who thought it perfectly fine to change her cats' litter box once a month. I couldn't see the truck driver through the glare of his lights, but hopefully he'd head out soon. If not, we'd have to move to the overnight parking lot before we suffocated. This was our fifth night at the Flying J, and I still didn't understand why truckers left their rigs running for hours at a time.

Still, the Flying J was way better than the Safeway parking lot which offered no bathroom overnight and had scary people roaming around. And it was a hundred times better than Wal-Mart, which did have twenty four hour access to a restroom for Aunt Junie and me, but not for Boone. The manager was so insulted over one little pile of poop on his pavement he threatened to call the police if we didn't leave. The sorry jerk wasn't smart enough to realize the loss was really his, because I would never spend even one penny of my money at any Wal-Mart ever again.

At least here at the Flying J we had a convenience store with a deli and sub shop, a fairly clean restroom with twelve stalls and even a shower if you paid $2.50 for a token. Even better, there was an empty lot full of nothing but gravel and weeds where Boone could do his business without anybody caring.

I zigzagged between the maze of rumbling trucks, across the blacktop fueling area, and over to the travel plaza. I hung around the glass doors for a few seconds to make sure nobody inside looked familiar. Aunt Junie said not to worry if the employees recognized us. As long as we bought stuff and didn't cause trouble, we could camp out as long as we wanted. But truck stops were for truckers who needed a rest or a meal, or for travelers who needed gas or coffee or a bathroom break. It was not a place to *camp out*. That's what the woods were for.

I made a beeline for the deli, glad the girl behind the counter was different than the one we'd bought hot cocoa from earlier. This one was a red head with a lip piercing and French manicured nails. The nails were cool—electric blue with white tips. But the lip ring reminded me of all the gross pictures of piercings gone wrong I'd seen on the Mayo Clinic's website.

I blended in with the people milling around the deli display case and tried not to drool over all the delicious looking food behind the glass. I wanted one of everything—golden chicken breasts, fried potato wedges, macaroni salad, glistening hot sausages. But it was the steaming vat of cheesy broccoli soup on a nearby counter that made my mouth water and brought a lump to my throat.

Cheesy broccoli had been Mom's very favorite soup. I'd made it by the Crock-Pot full when she was sick and Aunt Junie was too busy taking care of her to cook. Mom's recipe was amazingly creamy, cheesy and rich, and even though I knew the Flying J's version probably wasn't half as good, I wanted it anyway. I studied the waxed serving cups, trying to decide if I should buy one big cup for Aunt Junie and me to share or two smaller ones.

A little boy bumped the back of my legs as he raced to his mom with a root beer clutched in his hands. She gave a firm shake of her head and his smile dissolved into a furious scowl that made me giggle. I grabbed two of the small cups from the stack. Aunt Junie and I could each have our own, and Boone could lick them out afterwards without getting as much mess on his face.

The girl behind the counter snapped her gum at the lady with the little boy. "What can I get you, ma'am?"

"Half a pound of potato salad, please and ... " she paused to scoop up the little boy as he started crying, " ... a hot dog. Just plain."

I lifted the silver lid from the soup and carefully ladled a scoop, while the lady toted the little kid over to the cold

4

case and pointed out different kinds of fruit drinks. I felt a pinch of jealousy at the way he put his arm around his mom's neck. Sometimes I wished I could go back to being a little kid, when I had Mom to take care of me, and my biggest worry was whether or not *Dragon Tales* would be on that day.

I snapped the lid on the first cup and began to fill the second. The cashier popped her gum again and I wondered if it ever snagged on her lip ring. "What can I get you?" she asked the next customer.

"Two chicken breasts and a bean burrito please."

My arm jerked, and I nearly dropped the ladle.

I knew that voice!

The hair on the back of my neck stiffened just like Boone's when he saw another dog, and all kinds of crazy advice ran through my mind. *Run for your life if it's a brown bear, play dead if it's a grizzly.* Then I remembered where I was and decided just to freeze. It might have worked if not for the fat glob of cheesy broccoli that oozed over the side of the cup and burned my thumb. I licked it off fast and then turned my head just enough to glimpse the man's short cinnamon hair, the crisp blue uniform, the gun. I couldn't see his face, but I didn't need to. The deep, unhurried voice told me everything. It was Officer Murphy—our resource officer at Logan Elementary. How in the world could I have missed him?

It wasn't that I didn't like Officer Murphy. He patrolled the halls with a smile, and sometimes he'd even play kickball or tether ball during recess. But I'd also seen him put kids in handcuffs. And rumor had it he kept a jumbo box of tissues on his desk...and they weren't for him. I definitely didn't want to see him now, not when I had a bunch of unexcused absences.

Only a few yards separated us. He would turn any second. I considered a grab and dash with the soup, but the deli girl yelling, "Thief, thief!" would no doubt draw attention.

"Want any barbecue sauce?" she asked.

"No, thanks," he said. "I'll take sour cream if you've got that."

The red neon restroom light suddenly caught my eye, flashing like a rescue beacon. I edged toward it, one step, then two more.

"Shannon."

Pins and needles exploded across my scalp. I'd only made it three lousy steps. I did my best to look surprised as I wheeled around. "Oh...Officer Murphy, hi."

He broke into a smile. "Hey, there. Where've you been? Haven't seen you around school this week."

I patted my chest. "Oh, had a bad cold is all. Lots of congestion, you know." I was pleased with how normal my voice sounded. It was usually good to me that way. I could be pudding inside but my voice held solid.

"Yeah? Feeling better now?"

"Definitely." I bobbed my head harder than necessary.

"Good. I left a couple messages for your aunt Junie, but I never heard back."

I was already off kilter, but hearing him use Aunt Junie's name nearly pushed me clean off the scale. The two of them had talked when I registered for school, but still … the guy must have an amazing memory. "Oh, well, sometimes she forgets to check her messages."

"Ahh, gotcha." He glanced around. "Where is she anyway?"

"Out in the car." At least that much was true. I gestured at the soup. "I think I gave her my cold. She sent me in to grab dinner."

"Looks healthier than what I bought," he said. "Go ahead and pay for your stuff. I'll walk you out."

"Walk me out?" I echoed stupidly. "Um, like I said, I gave her my cold, so you might not wanna get too close."

He cocked an eyebrow, looking like he might laugh, and I felt like a complete dork. The guy got paid to keep order at an overcrowded school, to settle fights and deal with problems. He'd probably heard the very best stories from the very best liars, and I wasn't even close to being in that league. "Thanks for the warning," he said, "but I think I can hold my own."

An odd vibration started in the pit of my stomach, a lot like the soft clicking of the crickets back home. "Okay." I fumbled to snap the lid on the second soup cup and then crept to the counter.

7

"Is this gonna do it for you?" The cashier asked. "Need anything else?"

Yes, please, I wanted to beg. *I need you to find a way to keep this guy from following me out to the car, from finding out our secret.* But my tongue was stuck to the roof of my mouth and the best I could do was shake my head.

"All righty then, that'll be four twenty-six."

I could feel Officer Murphy's eyes on the back of my head. Aunt Junie was still in a stupor no doubt. She didn't know I'd taken the money or even left, and there'd be no chance to warn her. I stared at the cashier's lip ring, like maybe it would provide some kind of plan if only I studied it hard enough. But she handed me my change a few seconds later and I was out of time.

CHAPTER TWO

OFFICER MURPHY PUSHED open the glass door and waved me through. "Ladies first." He scanned the parking lot. "Where to?"

The White Freightliner had pulled out and I could just make out the black roof of Aunt Junie's Impala. "Over there."

"Why'd she park so far away?"

I shrugged. "Don't know. To stay out of the way of the trucks, I guess." Good thing we hadn't moved to the overnight lot yet, or he'd really think something weird was going on.

Boone stared out the back window like a little watchman. His ears flattened and his whole body wiggled with joy once he spotted me. *Bark,* I silently pleaded. *Bark really loud.* But of course he didn't. Dogs only barked when you didn't want them to.

Aunt Junie was still slumped against the driver's door, and I knew what I had to do. "Oh, look," I said, forcing a giggle. "She fell asleep."

I set the soup cups on the trunk and then gave the driver's side window a hard rap—a two second warning before I yanked the door part way open. "Hey, Aunt Junie. Surprise!"

Her body tilted toward me, and for a terrifying second I feared she might topple right out onto the pavement.

Officer Murphy must have thought so too, because he jumped forward, his arms thrust out. "Whoa," he said.

Aunt Junie gave a mighty snort and caught herself just in time. She jolted up, bug-eyed and hazy. "Huh...what?"

I touched her shoulder, feeling like a big jerk. "Sorry, Aunt Junie. I didn't know you were really asleep. But look...we have company." I kept my eyes glued to hers, praying she was awake enough to get my message. "I ran into Officer Murphy at the deli. He's from my school, remember?"

She focused on me, blinking. "What? Ohhh."

Officer Murphy stepped up beside me. "Hello there, Junie. How's it going?"

Boone took advantage of the open door and sailed into my arms with enough force to make me take a step back. He shivered with happiness when Officer Murphy tickled him under the chin. "Hey, pup," he said, "awesome leap. You must be part kangaroo."

"Yeah," I said, "he's a real doggaroo."

Officer Murphy laughed, and I felt immensely clever.

Aunt Junie rubbed her drooping cheeks. Her brown curls had escaped their bobby pins and stuck out at all angles. She made a show of smoothing them back before she grabbed her glasses off the dash and shoved them on her face. "So what are you doing here?" she snapped.

I did a double take.

Officer Murphy raised his paper bag from the deli. "Just getting a bite to eat. Shannon says you're not feeling so hot."

She frowned. "What? No, I'm … good."

I let out a soft breath. She didn't look good, she looked like she'd partied all night. But at least she was upright, and there were still traces of the eye shadow and liner she carefully applied each morning. She rubbed a knuckle below her eye like her mascara might have run. "I guess I drifted off. So what can I do for you?"

One corner of Officer Murphy's mouth curled up. "Nothing special. I just wanted to make sure you knew Shannon's missed the last several days of school. I left messages."

Her brown eyes swept over him. "Sorry," she said, like it was the last thing she meant. "I just get busy and forget to check my voice mail. But yeah, I know she's missed a few days. Is that a crime?"

He lost his smile. "She needs to be in school. It's the law."

I nervously scanned the Impala, trying to see things through Officer Murphy's eyes. My backpack lay unzipped in the back seat, along with my math book and the Top Raman container I used for Boone's water, but there wasn't anything that screamed out *homeless*. Our pillows, blankets, and clothes were all packed in the trunk, along with the food and other odds and ends like paper plates, can opener, dog food and bathroom stuff.

Officer Murphy glanced at me. Then he sniffed the air and frowned, as if he'd suddenly caught a whiff of Mrs. Zilinksy's place. He braced his hands on Aunt Junie's door and leaned toward her. "So, is it my imagination or do I smell alcohol?"

Aunt Junie seemed to come completely awake, eyes flashing behind her gold-rimmed glasses. "Is that really any of your business?"

I gaped at her, floored. There was something very strange going on here, something that gave me goosebumps.

Officer Murphy clicked his tongue. "If you were at home, no. But when you're sitting behind the wheel ... you bet it's my business."

"I don't drink and drive if that's what you're suggesting. I'm not that stupid, okay?"

"So, if I searched the car, I wouldn't find any open containers, right?"

The faintest blush colored Aunt Junie's cheeks, and I could see her brain stumbling for a response. But then she batted her eyes at him, as if she'd decided the best defense was to treat the whole thing like a joke. "And just why do you ask, Mr. Policeman? Do you have a search warrant?"

He didn't smile. "Don't mess with me, *ma'am.*"

Aunt Junie drew back a little, like she realized she was balancing on razor thin wire. "Sorry," she said. "I was just...being goofy. But no, there's no open containers inside the car."

Boone's little heart bump, bumped fast against my arm, keeping rhythm with my own, and I figured he knew as well as me she was lying. There wasn't any alcohol inside the car. But there was half a bottle of tequila in the trunk. Wasn't the trunk part of the car?

Officer Murphy hesitated. He glanced at me again, then back at Aunt Junie before he patted the door frame with the heel of his hand and straightened. "Okay," he said. "Okay." He winked at me. "You're gonna be in school tomorrow, right?"

"Oh, yeah," I said. "Definitely."

"Good," he said. "I'll look for you." He tipped his head at Aunt Junie. "Good to see you again. Take care."

"Yeah, you too," she mumbled.

Officer Murphy's gaze swept the Impala once more, then he ruffled Boone's ears before heading across the lot. "Hey, Shannon," he called back, "don't forget your food's on the trunk."

"Oh, yeah," I said, waving. "Thanks." I pushed Boone back inside the car and then handed Aunt Junie the soup before going around to open the passenger door. I slipped in and fell against the leather seat.

Aunt Junie rolled her head back and forth on the headrest. "Crap," she moaned. "That was way too close. What were you thinking, Shannon?"

The stress of the last few minutes flooded through me and I felt sick. "I'm sorry. I didn't know he'd be in there."

"Why didn't you wake me up before you went over?"

I blinked fast. "I tried. I'll wait for you next time, promise. I was just really hungry."

She glanced at the cups like she was noticing them for the first time. "Soup?"

I nodded. "Cheesy broccoli."

Her face softened. "Oh, bug." She set the soup on the flat section of the dash and closed her eyes. "I'm sorry, okay? It's not your fault. I'm totally the world's sorriest guardian ever."

"No you're not," I said. "Don't say stuff like that."

She smirked. "God, I can only imagine what Faye would say."

She was right. Mom would be crushed if she knew how things had gone downhill in the two years she'd been gone. But it wasn't Aunt Junie's fault. She was certified to cut hair and do nails, and she'd had a good job at the

14

Lotus Spa back home. Combined with Mom's earnings from Shopko we'd done fine.

Aunt Junie had planned to go back to school and get her esthetician certificate so she could do skin care and eyelash extensions too. She'd saved half the money she needed when Mom was diagnosed with cancer and had to quit her job. Then a year and a half later, Mom died, leaving Aunt Junie saddled with me. The money she'd saved for school had been spent trying to keep our house ... which we'd lost anyway. She might as well have taken her four thousand dollars and scattered it around the pot-holed streets of Plummer.

"You'll find a job soon," I said. "And Washington pays better than Idaho, right?"

Aunt Junie gave a solemn nod. "Yeah, but the state exams cost more too. Three hundred bucks. Guess I should've done a little more research."

Fear wormed its way into my stomach. "When did you find that out?"

"Last week."

"You should've told me."

She rolled her eyes. "Why, you have three hundred bucks stashed somewhere?"

I felt like she'd jabbed me with a piece of kindling. Of course I didn't have a solution. I was the problem. Not that she actually said that, but it's how she felt. I knew it as sure as I knew Officer Murphy's voice. If not for getting stuck with me, Aunt Junie would still be in Plummer, probably in a little apartment of her own, supporting herself just fine. I was the reason her paycheck wasn't enough. I was the reason we were living in a car.

She lightly brushed my arm with her fingertips. "Hey, forget it, okay? It is what it is." She puffed out a sigh. "I'll hold off on the licensing for now and start applying other places. Maybe at restaurants. At least there I could earn tips." She uttered the word *restaurants* like she'd bitten into a green apricot, and it left me feeling as worthless as a dull penny in a bag of shiny quarters.

My stomach filled the silence with a lion sized growl.

Aunt Junie laughed. "Holy cow, Shannon!" She reached for the soup cups and handed me one.

The warm Styrofoam felt good against my fingers, and the smell was even better. I peeled back the lid. "Oh, shoot," I groaned. "I forgot spoons."

Aunt Junie shrugged. "Who cares? Let's drink it."

I gave her a grateful smile. "Great idea." I raised my cup and drew in a big mouthful of the thick, golden soup. I could feel the warm film on my upper lip even before Aunt Junie grinned. "How is it?" she asked.

"Not quite as good as Mom's, but very yummy."

She nodded. "I don't suppose anybody could make it as good as your mom."

Boone whined, his bright, chocolate eyes riveted to my soup cup. He wiggled when I smiled at him. It was tough not to smile when you looked at Boone. Most of his body was white with polka dots of tan. But his face had a big square of dark brown over one eye that made him look like he was wearing a patch. Mom called him a little pirate.

She'd taken me to the animal shelter and let me pick him out one freezing morning in February. Then we'd brought him home and played with him on the braided rug in the living room, soaking up the toasty warmth of the wood stove. I remembered feeling so happy, like it was the most perfect day ever. Then out of the blue Mom broke down in tears and admitted she didn't expect to survive her cancer. And with those few words, my perfect day dissolved into the worst one ever. Boone was the last and the best gift she ever gave me. And in her final weeks, he'd been the only thing that pulled me through.

I scooped up a chunk of broccoli between my thumb and forefinger. "Aunt Junie, how come you acted like you were mad at Officer Murphy?"

She stiffened. "I didn't. He's just… I mean, the whole thing freaked me out is all. I was asleep, for Pete's sake."

I didn't get why she still sounded mad about it, but I only nodded. "I better get to school tomorrow."

"I know. I know."

"What do you think would happen if he finds out we're living in the car?"

"He won't, bug. You worry too much."

"But what if he did? Do you think he'd tell?"

She swiped a finger around the rim of her cup. "I suppose legally he'd have to report that kind of thing, yeah."

"They'd take me away from you," I said. "Just like Amber." I waited for her to tell me I was wrong, that she'd never allow something like that to happen. But she didn't. She didn't say anything at all. Which told me I was one hundred percent right.

Amber was my best friend all through first grade and part of second—until the day she vanished. At first I figured she was sick. But after a week I started to worry. I knew Amber's family hadn't gone on vacation or moved because her big brother still came to school. I pestered my teacher until she finally took me into the hall and quietly explained that Amber was in a challenging family situation and wouldn't be returning. I guess her explanation was supposed to make me feel better, but it didn't. All it did was make the whole situation more scary and mysterious—just like those unsolved crime mysteries Mom liked to watch.

I dreamed Amber had drowned, or been kidnapped, or gotten sucked into one of those black holes we learned about in science. I worried I might just up and disappear too. It wasn't until the end of second grade that I finally learned Amber had gone into foster care because she'd been abused. Even after four years I still worried about her, and I still hated mysteries. I never read them, and I didn't watch them on TV.

Boone broke into my thoughts with a soft whimper. His little pink tongue darted back and forth in anticipation and I could read his mind perfectly. I lowered the center console so he could jump on, and then offered my soup cup.

Aunt Junie ran a hand through her hair. "I'm doing the best I can, Shannon. You know that, right?"

"I know," I said, and I meant it. But her words left me hungry, like she'd waved a piece of warm huckleberry pie beneath my nose and yanked it away without giving me any, because she hadn't said any of the things I desperately needed to hear.

Everything's gonna be okay as long as we have each other. You're worth all the effort. I love you.

CHAPTER THREE

M Y HAIR WAS still wet when Aunt Junie drove me to school the next morning. She'd helped me wash it in one of the restroom's steel sinks, and not only had the water turned cold half way through, but the cleaning lady came in and huffily told us to buy a shower token. My neck still itched with shame. And it wasn't the kind of itch you could scratch either, because it wasn't on my skin, it was deep inside.

Aunt Junie pointed at the little dash clock as we pulled into the drop off lane at school. "Not only did I get you here, I got you here on time."

"Yahoo," I mumbled. I lifted Boone from my lap and kissed his soft muzzle. "Be a good boy, okay? I'll see you after school." Aunt Junie grabbed the scruff of his neck to keep him from lunging after me as I opened the door. "Hope you find a job today," I said.

She snorted. "Yeah. Wouldn't that be great?"

I made the mistake of watching Aunt Junie pull away. Boone stared at me through the passenger window, his tongue a thin line of pink between his lips. He only stuck out his tongue when he was super focused on me, and it took everything I had not to run after the car. I wished I could stick him in my backpack and keep him with me all day.

I hefted my pack over my shoulder and blended with the stream of kids flowing inside. I loved school back in Plummer. I got straight A's. But sometime over these past two months my feelings about school had become just another lost thread in the tangled ball of string that was my life.

I'd barely made it to my locker when a hand grabbed my elbow and I whirled into the wide, grinning face of Mitzi. "Hey you skipper, you're finally back. What happened to you?"

"Hey," I said, instantly relieved. Mitzi was the only kid at Logan who seemed to know I was alive. All the others swirled in their own busy orbit, staring through me or past me or above me like I didn't exist—which wasn't necessarily a bad thing. The less attention I got, the less people I had to fool.

Mitzi jumped back. "Ugh, your hair's wet."

I forced a laugh. "Hey, I was in a hurry this morning, okay? At least I'm here."

"I can't believe you missed the drug search last Friday. It was so cool. They brought in dogs, and four kids had pot in their locker, including… you'll never guess who?"

"Who?"

Mitzi bounced on her toes. "Ashley."

I thought for a minute before blinking in surprise. "Ashley Wright?"

She squealed. "Yes, can you believe it? It was so awesome. She's kicked out all this week."

I pictured Ashley in my mind. Petite, slender, celebrity pretty, and the biggest snob you could ever imagine. I was genuinely sorry I'd missed it. "How do you know it's for a week?"

"Cause Officer Murphy gave us a big lecture after the search. He told us all that stuff about… " she paused to drop her voice down deep, " … the consequences of bad decisions and the benefits of good ones."

Hearing Officer Murphy's name made my stomach cramp, but I managed a grin and a fist bump. "Awesome," I said. "I better be here for the next one."

"No kidding. Oh, and you missed the science quiz too."

"Yeah, yeah," I said. "I'll make it up." I kneeled to sort through my locker, trying to remember if today was an A or B day. I grabbed both my math and history books just to be on the safe side.

"So you never told me where you were," Mitzi said.

"Sick," I said, but I didn't look her in the face as the lie escaped. Feeling rumpled and dirty on the outside was bad enough. But lying to the only friend I had made me feel dirty on the inside too. And that was way worse.

Pole bean skinny Brian Frank ambled past, his nose in his cell phone, and ran smack into Mitzi. She gave an indignant yelp and put her hands on her hips. "Watch where you're going, rude dude."

He glanced up long enough to sneer at her. "Hey, it's not my fault your butt's so big it takes up half the hall."

Mitzi rolled her eyes like the slam hadn't bothered her, but I knew it had, and I wanted to say something to make her feel better. "Guess what I learned from my anatomy book?" I said. "It takes forty eight muscles to frown at someone, but only eleven muscles to slap them."

Mitzi's mouth formed an O before she burst out laughing. "Oh, man, that's epic."

I smiled. "Come on," I said, and we shouldered our way to Mrs. Stedman's class.

Mrs. Stedman was busy scrawling on the white board as I walked up to her desk. I cleared my throat to get her attention and she turned with a warm smile. "Shannon, hello. We missed you."

Her smile gave me a warm glow because Mrs. Stedman was not a fake person. You could believe what she said, and I liked honest people I could trust—which explained why I didn't like myself much lately. I handed her my note from Aunt Junie and she read it with a sympathetic cluck of her tongue. "Caught the creeping crud that's been going around, huh?"

"Yeah." It was only eight in the morning, and I'd already lied to two people who deserved better. What a spectacular way to start the day.

"Well, I'm glad you're back," Mrs. Stedman said. "Come see me during break and I'll go over your missed assignments with you, all right? We really need to get you caught up." She looked past me. "Tyler and Levi, please remove the ball caps. You guys know the rules."

I slipped over to my desk and my blue metal chair made an awful "screech" as I scooted it back. Mrs. Stedman had our desks arranged in a big semi-circle around her own. Mine was farthest on the left, below the *Turn Knowledge into College* poster. Mitzi sat on the opposite end, next to the colorful bins where we turned in assignments, so we could pretty much look straight across at each other.

She caught me looking now and quickly pulled her upper body into a muscle man pose. I giggled. I couldn't help it. And I suddenly realized just how glad I was to be back at school where I could pass myself off as normal, where I could almost forget that Aunt Junie and Boone and I were living in our car. But then I spotted the brown trail of cocoa dribbled across the bottom of my T-shirt and my face flushed with horror. I quickly tugged up the zipper on my sweatshirt.

Aunt Junie and I were in desperate need of a trip to the laundromat. We'd been washing out underwear in the Flying J restroom late at night, hanging them over the headrests to dry. But my jeans stunk of diesel, and I was wearing the cleanest of my dirty shirts—or at least it had been before I spilled cocoa on it. I'd have to make another sneaky visit to the lost and found box.

The bell rang and there was a rush of sneakers and boots as everyone scrambled to their desks. "Morning boys and girls," Mrs. Stedman said. "You should already be in your seats by now."

Luke took a flying leap for his chair and missed by at least a foot. He tucked and rolled before popping back to his feet and the class howled with laughter. Even Mrs. Stedman laughed. "A move worthy of a gymnast," she said.

Luke grinned and took a bow. "Thank you, all."

Mrs. Stedman held up her hands until the hubbub died down. "Okay, everybody. Let's get attendance out of the way so we can dive in. We've got a great day ahead of us." She quickly ran through her checklist of names and then tore the page from her clipboard. "Does anyone know where Lara is today? She's supposed to be my student aide . . . no? Okay, who wants to fill in and take the attendance to Officer Murphy?"

I scrunched in my chair as her eyes swept the room. When they fell on me I quit breathing. But then Levi raised his hand. "I'll go."

"Wonderful, Levi, thank you," Mrs. Stedman said. She handed him the paper. "And maybe while you're with Officer Murphy you could explain to him why you insist on wearing your hat even after you were told to remove it."

Levi whipped off his cap with an innocent look. "Whoops," he said, and the class laughed again.

"That's better," Mrs. Stedman said. "Hurry back." She surveyed the room. "We still have a couple of students who haven't taken Friday's science test so I won't be handing them back quite yet. But there's some great scores in there, so wonderful job everyone." She pointed to the clock. "We've got thirty minutes to finish our unit on major historical time periods, and then we've got two more guests coming in to speak with us about careers."

There was a murmur of approval from the class, and I wondered if I'd missed any guests while I'd been absent. I hoped not, because I liked hearing about different kinds of jobs. Last week we'd had a pediatrician, which was my favorite visit so far since I wanted to be a doctor. Not a kids' doctor, though. I was going to be a cancer doctor—an oncologist, so I could find a cure for the kind of cancer that took Mom. And while I was busy accomplishing that, I'd make a ton of money and win a lot of awards that I'd use to decorate the walls of my clinic. All the other doctors

would consult me when they ran into a tough case. I'd be
the specialist everyone looked up to.

Mitzi's hand shot up. "Who's coming this time, Mrs.
Stedman?"

"I've invited a friend of my husband's to talk about
home construction. And Bethany's mother is going to tell
us about her work as an esthetician."

Mitzi's eyebrows formed a squiggle. "A what?"

"A skin care specialist," I said, without planning to.
Sometimes my mouth did that, spoke without telling
me first.

Twenty four sets of eyes zeroed in on me, and I raised
my chin. "It's what my aunt wants to do."

Bethany clamped her lips in a pout, as if I'd taken the
attention away from her, but our teacher smiled. "Excellent,
Shannon." And I gave a gracious nod.

Mrs. Stedman passed out worksheets on the Renaissance
and asked us to imagine being twelve years old in Elizabethan
England. I tried, but history wasn't my favorite, and the longer I listened the foggier my brain got, until my eyes drifted
closed a time or two. It had been a while since I'd slept clear
through the night. Trying to rest in the backseat of a car
was a lot like tent camping without a mattress—bumpy and
uncomfortable. Plus, the Flying J was just plain noisy. Trucks
ran their compression units, doors slammed, people yakked
on their phones. Boone didn't help either. At least twice a
night he tunneled out of my sleeping bag to bark—like last

night, when the casino bus parked beside us, and fifty some people stumbled past at three in the morning.

I jabbed my wrist with the tip of my pencil to stay awake as Mrs. Stedman talked, but once her husband's construction worker friend, Mr. Henry, showed up, I caught my second wind. It's tough to ignore an old guy with white braided hair and bright red suspenders. He held up photos of different types of homes he'd built, and my head swam with homesickness when he showed us a log cabin just like our little house in Plummer.

Our cabin had white adobe between the logs, creaky old oak floors, and a wood stove that pumped out so much heat we sometimes opened windows in the dead of winter. My bedroom overlooked a grove of quaking aspen that danced and trembled with the slightest breeze, and there were always deer, or turkey or a coyote passing through the woods out back.

It was the only home I'd ever known. Mom and Aunt Junie bought it together—right after Mom told her boyfriend he was going to be a dad, and he decided I wasn't worth knowing and split. Most of our stuff was still there, stored in the shed out back. But the shed wasn't weather proof, or mouse proof, and I wondered if our things would be any good by the time we found a new home.

A gasp yanked me from my daydreams, and I looked up to see Mr. Henry holding up his forefinger, which was nothing but an inch long stub. He told us how he'd lost it to a skill saw due to a second of distraction. The air filled with moans and Grace turned a shade of green that cracked everybody up. Then it was time for Mr. Henry to move on and Bethany's mom arrived.

Mrs. Fosberg was tall and slender, her wispy hair cut in layers, and wore a swirly red dress. She waited patiently while Mrs. Stedman introduced her and then flashed us a bright smile. "Okay, who knows what an esthetician does? Big, fancy word, I know."

Everyone looked at me, including Bethany, who narrowed her eyes. I still wasn't sure what I'd done to upset her, but the last thing I needed was enemies so I kept my mouth shut. Abby raised her hand with a smug look. "Something to do with skin care?"

"Right on," Mrs. Fosberg said. "An esthetician is a skin care and makeup specialist, and it fits under the broader career of cosmetology. I work at the Wildflower Spa," she continued. "I do facials and body treatments, eye lash extensions, skin analysis, waxing…"

Abby's hand shot back up. "And nails? My mom has her nails done every month."

"Absolutely," Mrs. Fosberg said. "Manicures and pedicures. You know what I really do," she said, smiling, "is make people feel better about themselves, make them feel beautiful. It's what I love most about my job."

A lump wedged itself into my throat, so big I could barely swallow, because I knew exactly what she meant.

And all of a sudden I wasn't sitting in Mrs. Stedman's class. I was at home, sitting on the end of Mom's rented hospital bed, playing beauty shop with her and Aunt Junie. We played it a lot during Mom's last months, after her hair had fallen out from all the chemo and she felt ugly.

Aunt Junie knew just how to use Mom's favorite shade of coral green eye shadow to make her hazel eyes dance again. How to use rose blush to bring the pink back to Mom's cheeks. How to use colorful head scarves to make her feel beautiful again. Then she'd dab Pink Teaser lip gloss on me, and French braid my hair, and we would wear scarves to match Mom's. And before long, Mom would be smiling again. It was like magic—magic only Aunt Junie could perform.

"Are there any jobs open at your spa?" I asked, forgetting to raise my hand. "My aunt does hair and nails, she just needs to get certified."

Mrs. Fosberg's red lips formed a square. "She can't expect to find work at any spa without being certified."

There was a smattering of snickers from the class and my cheeks flamed. "I know that," I said. "She has her certification in Idaho, she just needs to get it for Washington."

"Well, it's true," Mrs. Fosberg said, "each state has its own requirements." She gave a small shrug. "But it's no big deal to get licensed in another state. It shouldn't cost more than a few hundred dollars for your aunt to pass her tests here."

Anger blazed through me like a forest fire through pine, and I struggled to keep my face straight. How dare she stand there with her swirly red dress and high heels and act like a few hundred dollars was nothing. Because when you were living in a car and your closet was a trash bag, a few hundred dollars was a fortune. I tried not to think about all the money Aunt Junie used to have saved up. The money she'd probably still have if not for me.

Abby raised her hand. "How much does it cost to become an esthetician?"

"It depends on the school," Mrs. Fosberg said. "But the average is around five thousand dollars."

Mrs. Stedman pointed to the *Turn Knowledge into College* poster above my head and said, "Boys and girls, never be put off by the cost of higher education. Almost all schools offer some sort of financial aid—loans, scholarships, grants, something. Remember what I always say, where there's a will, there's a way."

I thought about it as my anger cooled into something more like disappointment. I didn't know anything about financial aid, surely Aunt Junie had looked into that type of thing. But the whole pitch about *where there's a will, there's a way* was nothing but a big pile of bologna. After all, I had a powerful will for lots of stuff—to be someone's most treasured thing, to have a home, for Aunt Junie to find a good job. But what good was having a will, when the way seemed as far out as another galaxy?

CHAPTER FOUR

I WAS STILL PONDERING what Mrs. Stedman said about schools offering financial help when she passed out our iPads after lunch. "Absolutely no talking during your reading quiz," she reminded. "And if you get done early, you can use the time to catch up on any missed assignments or to do other quiet work."

I breezed through my quiz in only ten minutes and then ran a search for cosmetology schools. I was surprised to see three different results pop up within fifteen miles of us. The Logan School of Beauty was only ten blocks away. I clicked to the school's financial aid page, but after only a minute I got bogged down with stuff I didn't understand.

I couldn't find any financial aid page for the second school. But there was all kinds of links for the third place— the Silver Heart Academy of Cosmetology. I wondered what a Silver Heart Essay Award was. It was such a cool sounding name. I clicked the link.

Silver is considered by most to be inferior to gold, both in value and beauty. But those of us here at the Silver Heart Academy of Cosmetology respectfully disagree. We happen to consider silver every bit as special and beautiful as gold. In like manner, we do not consider a person facing difficult life circumstances to be inferior in any way to someone who has never had to struggle or exert great effort to achieve something.

Our school was founded in 1972, by Thomas and Marjorie Silver—a couple who began with nothing, and who struggled mightily to establish this school and make it what it is today—a renowned institution of cosmetology and design—a Better Business Pick ten years in a row. It is respect and appreciation for this effort that marked the establishment of the Silver Heart Essay Award—a semiannual grant awarded to three deserving students who, through no fault of their own, are unable to finance a degree in cosmetology. Recipients of the grant receive tuition covering our standard four month course, as well as either the six week nails or waxing course. Job placement assistance is also provided. For more information please click here

A slow, tingling fear seeped through me as I stared at the more information link. I knew a whole lot about feeling inferior, so I loved that bit about silver being as important as gold, but Mrs. Fosberg had already crushed my hopes once today, I was afraid to click the link and have it happen again. Besides, Mom always told me if something sounded too good to be true it probably was. And this definitely sounded too good to be true. Still, if there was a catch, I might as well find out what it was.

The Silver Heart Essay is exactly that—an essay, to be no more than 1,000 words, typed, or neatly hand written, introducing yourself and explaining why you believe you deserve to be a recipient of the Silver Heart Essay Award. Special attention should be given to describing your interest in the field of cosmetology, as well as what kind of difficulties prevent you from achieving your goal. Each school session we receive at least fifty applicants—let us know what makes you different than the rest.

Good Luck and Warm Wishes
The Silver Heart Academy of Cosmetology

By the time I finished reading, my insides weren't just warm they were almost melting with possibility. Could it be real, or was it just a trick? I gnawed on a fingernail. If it was real, and if I could make it happen, it could change everything for me and Aunt Junie. She could get the extra training she wanted, she could find a good job doing what she loved. But way more important than that, I'd be the one to fix things for us. I'd go from a burden to a hero. From a dull penny to a shining quarter. No, forget the quarter, I'd be worth my weight in gold. It was all I could do not to jump up from my chair and do a victory lap.

I wondered how much an esthetician in Washington earned. I stole a glance at Bethany. She wore a pretty floral top over cuffed jeans and bright blue Van sneakers. I didn't know where she lived, but it was a pretty safe bet it was someplace with four walls and not four wheels.

My mind danced off to all the things I could buy if Aunt Junie and I had money—a whole grocery cart full of peanut butter, cheese, apples, ice-cream and dog food. A whole bag of rawhide chews and toys for Boone. A new winter coat for me, plus some of those super cute combat boots like Mitzi wanted. I'd buy two pairs of the charcoal leather ones with the fancy gold buckles so we could match. And if there was any money left over, I'd buy...

"Boys and girls," Mrs. Stedman's voice suddenly boomed into my thoughts. "We'll be collecting the iPads soon, so please finish up your reading quiz if you haven't already done so."

I waited until her back was turned before whipping out my phone to take a picture of the site. I needed time to reread everything, to convince myself it was real and not some crazy dream. It would give me something to do tonight when I couldn't sleep.

I waited on the sidewalk after school, searching the mile long line of cars for a black topped Chevy Impala with an adorable little dog in the window. I switched my pack from shoulder to shoulder, repeatedly checking my phone for messages and trying not to think the worst. Aunt Junie was probably just further back in line than normal. Maybe she was stuck in traffic or had stopped for gas. Maybe ... just maybe, she'd found a job and forgotten the time. I'd forgive her for that. No, I'd hug her for that.

But by three-fifty the line of cars in the pick-up lane had dwindled to a dozen, and my toes were numb from the cold sidewalk. It was illegal to use your cell phone while driving in Washington, but maybe Aunt Junie wasn't driving anyway, maybe she'd plain forgotten me. It was time to call. I curled and uncurled my free hand as I counted the rings, afraid it might go to voice mail. But finally ... Aunt Junie picked up.

"Helloooo," she said, her voice as thick as molasses.

The relief drained right out of me. "Aunt Junie, it's me. Are you and Boone okay?"

"Oh, hi bug. I'm gooood."

"Then where *are* you? It's almost four o'clock."

There was a long pause. "Almost four," she repeated, like I'd shared some interesting bit of trivia. "Hmm, I guess ... OHHHH," she said, and I knew she finally got it. "Almost four! Oh, geeeeez, Shannon. I must have fallen asleep."

My stomach squeezed with fear. "Aunt Junie," I whispered, taking a quick look over my shoulder at the mostly empty sidewalk. "Have you been drinking?"

"Whaaaat? Oh, I'm great. I'm on my way right now."

She hadn't answered my question, but I already knew the answer. "Be careful, okay? Drive real careful."

I trudged over to the stone planter near the door to the sixth grade wing. The freezing concrete seeped through my jeans and made me all the colder. What was Aunt Junie thinking? She was supposed to be looking for a job, not taking a stupid nap in the middle of the afternoon—and definitely not drinking. She'd always liked tequila. From the time I was a little kid I remembered her having a shot when she got home from work, and another before bed. It helped her unwind, she said, helped her sleep better.

One shot at a time had become two after Mom died. It hadn't felt like a big deal then, but now it felt huge. A bottle of Milagro tequila from Pirelli's Liquor store cost $23.99 with tax—the receipt for the last bottle was still in the glove box—and she bought a new one each week. We didn't have money for that sort of thing right now. We didn't have money for *anything* right now. And what about

37

Boone? He was stuck riding around with her. If she did something stupid and hurt him, I'd never forgive her. The more I thought about it the more it steamed me.

The hall door clanked open, and I instantly grabbed my phone and pretended to text. I wanted to look like a girl with a purpose—not a girl who'd been forgotten by her aunt.

Black shoes caught my attention. Loafers with laces, not the kind a kid would wear. My thumbs froze over the keyboard.

"Hey, Shannon."

I glued on a happy face. "Oh … hi, Officer Murphy."

"What's up?"

"Nothing. Just waiting for my aunt."

"A little late, huh?"

I squeezed out a giggle. "Yep. Sometimes she gets busy and forgets the time."

He crossed his arms. "Where's your coat? You just got over being sick."

"In my locker," I said, which was true. I didn't add that I only wore it when I had to because it was last year's and the sleeves were embarrassingly short.

"It's thirty some degrees."

I willed my teeth not to chatter. "Really? Doesn't feel that cold."

He sat down on the planter next to me, so close I was sure he'd be able to hear my heart pounding. I did my best to lean away without actually moving. "How was the soup?" he asked.

"The soup?" My mind stumbled. "Ohhhh. It was awesome, really good. Cheesy broccoli," I added.

He smiled. "I'm a minestrone guy myself."

"That's the kind with the pasta and beans, right?"

"Yep. My mom used to make it for me when I was sick."

"Nice." I didn't have a clue what else to say. All I knew was that he needed to be gone by the time Aunt Junie showed up. If not, he might talk to her again. He'd smell the tequila for sure. I could practically smell it over the phone.

My stomach suddenly let out one of its famous grumbles—a really long, thunderous one that sounded like a herd of elephants and made me want to die of humiliation.

He chuckled. "Must be our talk about food, huh?"

"I'm always hungry after school."

"I don't know any kid who's not."

He stood then, and I was so relieved, until he said, "Come with me."

The back of my neck prickled. "Um ... I better stay out here and watch for Aunt Junie. She should be here any time."

He'd reached the door by then, and he looked back at me and motioned. "Yeah, I know. It'll only take a minute."

I gripped the cold concrete of the planter. I didn't want to go with him, I wanted to stay right here where I felt safe.

But I wasn't sure how to tell him that, or even if I could. Were you allowed to say no to a police officer? "Okay, sure," I said.

Funny how much wider the hallway seemed without a bunch of kids racing around like NASCAR. The custodian steered a push broom across the faded tile floor, keys jangling from a metal ring clipped to his belt. And Mrs. Baxter, one of the fifth grade teachers, tore sheets of craft paper from a giant roll outside her classroom. She looked up with a questioning smile and I wondered if she thought I was in trouble for something.

My mind was as numb as my toes by the time Officer Murphy stopped in front of the big vending machine outside the teacher's lounge. He dug a handful of change from his pocket. "Anything look good?"

I blinked. Was he for real? It all looked delicious. I glanced up at him, hesitating, and he smiled. "Well, what's it gonna be?"

"Sun Chips ... please."

He pushed a button for the chips and another for a flavored water. I thought the drink must be for him, but he scooped both snacks from the tray and handed them to me. "Here you go."

I couldn't believe it. I wondered if he'd ever bought snacks for any of the other kids. "Um ... wow, thanks."

He winked. "You're welcome."

I stood awkwardly for a few seconds, feeling like I should say something more. But what else was there to say? "Maybe I better go wait for my aunt now."

"Maybe you better," he said.

"Thanks, again." I headed back down the hall until I was out of Officer Murphy's sight before making a quick detour to the overflowing lost and found box. I set my snacks on the floor and pawed through the orphaned shirts, hats and jackets. There was some really cute stuff, but I was careful to pick only basic, hard to identify clothes in case the real owner happened to recognize something. I stuffed a pale blue T-shirt and a pair of black leggings under my sweatshirt before hurrying back out to the planter.

I savored each salty, cheesy Sun Chip, letting it sit on my tongue until it dissolved. The bag was empty by the time Aunt Junie finally turned into the pickup lane, and I felt the vibrating bass of the radio as she cruised to a stop. She'd made it ... safely.

Boone's eager little face was plastered against the window, and he started yipping when he spotted me. I dove in and grabbed him. "Hey, boy! How are you? I missed you." I laughed as he washed my face with kisses.

Aunt Junie grimaced. "That's disgusting to let him lick your face like that."

The smell of tequila reached me as I leaned to turn the radio down, and I was sorely tempted to tell her the smell was way more disgusting than Boone. I frowned into her red rimmed eyes. "Where were you, Aunt Junie? School got out an hour ago."

"I told you. I must have drifted off."

"But how could you fall asleep? I thought you were looking for a job."

She gave me a sour look. "I was, Shannon, all day ... or at least until one o'clock, or so. I was sitting in the car filling out an application for Ida's Bakery, and I just fell asleep. I was tired okay?"

"But how come you were drinking? Nobody will hire you."

"Hey, I don't need a lecture from you, okay?"

I hugged Boone against me and tried to swallow back my anger. "Can we just go?"

Aunt Junie stepped on the gas and the Impala gave a hard lurch as we pulled away from the curb. "Sheez," I yelped, bracing a hand against the dash.

"Crap," Aunt Junie said. "Sorry."

I glanced toward the school, relieved nobody was there to see. But then something dark blue caught my eye, and I recognized the familiar figure of Officer Murphy, watching through the window next to the door of the sixth grade hall.

CHAPTER FIVE

"WHERE ARE WE going?" I asked, a few minutes later. "The Flying J's the other way."

Aunt Junie tightened her grip on the steering wheel. "We're not going back to the truck stop. I'm sick of being cold at night. And it's impossible to get any rest when I have to warm up the stupid car every few hours so we don't freeze. Besides," she added, "it wastes gas having to drive you back and forth to school."

My stomach plunged. I worked my fingers into Boone's fur and tried not to overreact. "Okay. So then where are we going?"

She didn't answer as we wove our way through two more intersections and swung left a few blocks later. I was about to repeat my question for the third time when she pointed ahead of us. "Right there, that's where we're going."

I followed her finger to a large two story house with faded gray paint and a metal roof. "Who lives there?"

"It's a women's and children's shelter."

I stared at her, horrified. "What? You mean like ... a *homeless* shelter?" I could barely spit the word out.

Aunt Junie rolled her eyes. "Yes," she said, "a homeless shelter. Because right now, Shannon, that's what we are ... homeless."

I felt a little piece of my heart crack and drop away. We weren't truly homeless. We had a car and food. Homeless shelters were for people who had nothing, who were broke and desperate. People whose only other option was a park bench or an abandoned building. We were not like those people. "But we have a car," I whispered.

Aunt Junie pulled into the small gravel lot behind the house and parked. She twisted toward me with a pained look. "Yes, I'm thankful we have a car, but I'm sick of sleeping in it. This place has a bathroom so we can use the shower without paying, doesn't that sound fantastic? A hot shower instead of trying to wash up out of a sink? And it probably has a washing machine and dryer too. And beds. Wouldn't you love to stretch out for a change? It's like a motel."

I stared out at the miserable gray building and tried not to gag on the bitter taste lodged in my throat. She didn't understand. A place like this was nothing like a motel. When you checked into a motel, people didn't think anything bad about you, they assumed you were travelling. But a homeless shelter? People would *know*. They would look down on us, pity us. I would die a thousand deaths if anyone from school saw me in a place like this. And Aunt Junie was willing to risk it for a stupid shower and a bed?

I remembered listening to a radio show once, where the host asked people if they'd be willing to give up a hand or a foot in exchange for a million dollars. I was fascinated that four of the ten callers actually said yes. At the time I'd thought they were crazy. But now ... now I wasn't so sure.

But then I looked at Aunt Junie's expression. She looked more than tired, she looked broken and exhausted, with worry lines etched across her forehead that hadn't been there in Plummer. Lines that were there because of me. "Fine," I muttered. "If you really want to."

Aunt Junie bit her bottom lip. "Maybe just for a couple nights, okay?" She tapped her thumbs on the steering wheel. "But ... there is one thing about staying here I know you won't like."

"Only one thing?" I said, a weak attempt at a joke.

"They don't allow pets."

I sucked in a breath. "Are you kidding me? I'm not staying here if Boone can't."

"He can stay here, he just can't go inside. He'll have to sleep in the car."

"By himself? All night?"

Aunt Junie gripped the steering wheel hard enough to turn her knuckles white. "He's a dog, Shannon. It's not like he's scared of the dark."

"But … he'll get cold."

"He'll be fine. His fur is thick, and you can leave him a blanket."

"But he'll be scared. He's used to sleeping with me."

Aunt Junie smacked the steering wheel hard enough to stun me into silence. Her eyes blazed. "He'll. Survive. It's that, or he's gonna have to go to the animal shelter."

If I'd have been standing, her words would've knocked me flat. Boone met my eyes and whined softly. I didn't cry very often, but the way he lowered his ears like he knew we were talking about him made me tear up. "How can you even say something like that?"

Aunt Junie wilted like a punctured balloon. "Don't you get it, Shannon? Don't you see what a mess we're in? Having a dog only makes things harder. And guess who's stuck taking care of him all day while you're in school? Now I know you love him, but right now he's nothing but a—"

I clamped my hands over Boone's ears. "Stop," I hissed. "Don't you dare say it."

Now it was Aunt Junie's turn to look stunned. "Say what?"

"That he's a burden," I whispered. "Just like me."

She paled. "No … Shannon, that's not … I don't think you're a burden."

Tears tickled my cheeks, and I tried to nudge them off with my shoulder. "Yes you do," I said, "and that's okay. I get it, Aunt Junie. I know you didn't plan on getting stuck with me. But Boone is not a burden." I took a deep breath and choked back my tears. "He's my best friend, and he's the only part of Mom I have left."

There was another reason Boone was so special, a third reason every bit as important as the first two. Boone's love was one hundred percent for real—he loved me because he wanted to, not because he felt he should. But that was not the kind of thing you said out loud.

Aunt Junie put a hand to her forehead and slumped back against her seat. Neither of us spoke for what felt like a long time. Boone wiggled free of my grasp. He put his front legs on the arm rest and gazed out the window at a leafless young tree shifting in the wind. I swore it was shivering.

"You know," Aunt Junie said, her voice raspy, "sometimes it's really hard for me to look at you, Shannon. Because when I do, all I see is my sister. And I think how much I miss her, and how I'm completely failing in the one thing she asked me to do."

I swallowed. "I miss her too," I said, "all the time. But you're not failing. You just need to find a job, and then everything will be okay again. How much money do we need to get into an apartment?"

She sniffed. "You really wanna know? At least two thousand dollars."

I was shocked. "Two thousand dollars?" I echoed. "Rent is that much?"

"No. Rent is about eight hundred a month. But in order to move into an apartment you have to cough up the first and last month's rent, plus a cleaning deposit."

"The last month's rent? Why?"

"So if people decide to suddenly move out without paying, the landlord already has the money for that month. And the cleaning deposit is so if the tenants leave a big mess behind or do damage, then the landlord has money to fix it."

"Wow," I said, softly.

"Yeah," Aunt Junie agreed, her voice lifeless. "Wow."

I spent a few more minutes trying to wrap my head around that enormous sum and still couldn't. "Well," I finally said, "while we're getting stuff figured out, I think we need to stick together. All three of us. Mom would want us to. So if you really wanna stay here tonight, it's okay. I'll sleep out here with Boone."

She shook her head as a puzzled smile crept across her face. "So, let me get this straight. You'd really rather stay in the car in the cold with your dog, than stay someplace indoors with heat and a shower?"

I paused for half a breath, because it did sound pretty crazy when she put it that way. But then I looked at Boone, and I knew he was worth a hand or a foot ... or both. "Yep."

Aunt Junie rubbed her forehead. "Fine, bug. But I really, really need a decent night's sleep for a change. So what do you say we go get checked in and see what's what. Then you can come back out later if you really think you need to."

My insides crumbled. I hoped if I pushed her right to the edge, she'd give in and say we could go back to the Flying J. But instead, she'd called my bluff. She was truly picking a shower and a bed over me and Boone. My heart suddenly felt too big for my chest, but I set my face to stone so she wouldn't see. "Fine," I said. "Let's go."

We tromped up a wheel chair ramp and into a lobby that was half living room, half office. It reeked of cigarette smoke, greasy food and unwashed people. A boney woman sat on a metal folding chair reading a newspaper. She had hair like a haystack, held off her face with a black headband. "Howdy," she said, smiling. Both her front teeth were missing, just like a first grader's. I edged closer to Aunt Junie.

A heavy woman with bouncy gray curls glanced up from behind a desk. Her hair looked a lot happier than she did. "Evening. What can I do for you?"

Aunt Junie introduced herself. "We spoke on the phone earlier today."

The woman studied us without introducing herself back. A little plastic sign on her desk said Sue Moore. I guess she thought the sign was good enough. "I talk to a lot of people. Please remind me."

Aunt Junie opened her mouth, then paused as footsteps thumped overhead and ugly language drifted down with them. I wanted to high tail it out of there, back to the safety of the car and the Flying J. But I stayed put, rocking from foot to foot, wishing I had a mask to hide my identity.

The lady said, "uh, huh," several times as she listened to Aunt Junie, and I wondered if she suffered from a phobia of long words. There was actually a medical term for that, it started with the letters h-i-p-p-o and had at least eight more. The lady never smiled either. Not once. And I figured her smile muscles got about as much exercise as the rest of her. "How old are you?" she asked me, once Aunt Junie finished speaking.

"Twelve."

"Are you in school?"

"Yeah."

She shifted her gaze back to Aunt Junie. "Are you her legal guardian?"

"Yes. Ever since my sister, her mom, died two years ago."

"Dad's not in the picture?"

I felt a jolt.

"Excuse me?" Aunt Junie said.

"Her father," the lady said, sounding impatient. "He's not trying to get custody or anything?"

Aunt Junie's eyebrows drew together. "Oh, no, he's not around. He's not even … "

"Good." She seemed to relax. "You have no idea what a problem that is for us."

Right then is when I started to hate her. What kind of adult tells a kid it's a good thing her dad's not in the picture?

"Was sure a problem for me," the skinny woman on the chair blurted. "Sure was. Had some bad times and lost my kids. But I'm doin' better now. Gettin' clean, maybe take some classes, gonna get my babies back."

Sue frowned. "We're happy for you, Louise. But not everyone wants to hear your life story."

I felt embarrassed for the rude way Louise had been treated, but she didn't seem to mind.

"Anyway," Sue said, looking back at Aunt Junie, "you came at a good time. A room just became available."

Two amazingly dumb comments in a row. Did she really think there was a *good* time to show up at a homeless shelter?

"We offer rooms on a weekly basis," she continued. "Breakfast is at seven, dinner at six. No lunch."

"Food's not bad," Louise said, giving me a wink. "Especially the scrambled eggs. You like eggs, honey?"

"Louise," Sue snapped. "Either stop interrupting or leave the lobby."

"Sorry," Louise said, giving a gracious nod. "Sorry."

"The meals are on a donation basis, but you're not required to donate if you truly can't. But you *are* required to follow the rules." She held up a fat finger as she recited each one. "No males over ten years old are allowed on the premises. No smoking in the rooms. No alcohol. No pets. No loud talking or other noise after ten pm." She fixed Aunt Junie with a smug look. "If you have a problem with any of those it would be best to leave right now."

Aunt Junie hung her head like a little kid in trouble. "No problems," she muttered.

I thought of what I'd told Mitzi, how it only took eleven muscles to slap somebody, and I laced my fingers together so they'd have something else to do.

Sue trudged upstairs, down a narrow hallway, and past several closed doors with chipped, peeling paint. One had a hole down low like it had been kicked, another had a rainbow painted with chalk. She pointed out the bathroom as we walked by. "It's a shared bathroom," she said. "Limit your shower to ten minutes so everybody has an opportunity. The towels are in a cabinet right inside." She stopped before a closed door at the end of the hall, unlocked it, and then stepped aside so we could enter.

The room had a twin size bed, a roll away cot with blankets, a green corduroy recliner with a rip in the cushion, a small TV, coffee table, sink and a mini fridge. It was a lot bigger than the Impala, but smaller than a motel room.

"There's extra blankets beneath the cot," Sue said, pointing. "Oh, and one more thing, I try to screen the residents as best I can, but don't turn your back for one minute on anything you value, and always keep your door locked even when you're in the room. Things have a way of turning up missing around here."

My heart seized up. What about Boone? Jack Russell's were worth a lot of money. What if somebody stole him? All they'd have to do was break a window. He was so friendly, if they talked sweet he wouldn't even put up a fight.

"How many residents are there?" Aunt Junie said.

"Twenty-six at the moment, our max is thirty." She finally smiled. "Like I said, you showed up at a good time."

Aunt Junie raised her eyebrows. "Lucky us," she said.

CHAPTER SIX

T HE HEAVY SCENT of roast beef wafted into my nose as Aunt Junie and I found our way downstairs to dinner. A paper plate with *dining room* scrawled in black marker was taped to the wall outside the entrance, but the name was way too fancy for the room if you asked me. At least twenty people sat on benches lining both sides of a long, plastic covered table. Several women ate with babies balanced on their laps. One lady had a little kid tied with a leash to her belt, and another wore only a bathrobe. The only spot left to sit was at the end, next to a woman wearing army boots and a duct taped camo coat. The whole scene made my skin crawl.

I glanced at Aunt Junie, to see if she was anywhere near as panicked as me, but she seemed to be more interested in the stained linoleum floor than anything else. She nudged my arm. "You sit," she said. "I'll stand beside you." I would much rather have been the one to stand, but I swung a leg over the bench and balanced as near the end as I could without falling off.

Besides the roast beef, dinner was mushy carrots, half an orange and corn bread with butter. The food didn't taste bad, but the woman in the army boots smelled like she hadn't taken a shower in a month, and she kept mumbling to her food like she expected it to talk back. Then her plastic fork snapped in half and she laughed so hard she spewed cornbread crumbs in a two foot radius. I jumped up with a clenched stomach, afraid if I took another bite I'd throw up.

After we ate, Aunt Junie and I trudged back upstairs to the bathroom. The mirror was steamy from the last shower and there was more hand soap slopped across the counter than there was in the bottle. A pair of lacy red underwear lay on the floor, and Aunt Junie kicked them under the sink. "You can go first," she said, pulling a towel out of the cabinet for me. "I'll knock on the door when the ten minutes are up."

The shower curtain was nothing but a clear plastic liner and my muscles got all quivery at the thought of taking off my clothes in this strange place. "Will you wait in the hallway for me?"

"The door locks, bug."

I thought I might cry. "Please, Aunt Junie. Stay here and make sure nobody tries to come in."

She nodded wearily. "Okay. I'll wait."

I locked the door and undressed. The tub had a suspicious layer of grayish grime, and I spread out a washcloth before stepping in. Aunt Junie had been right about one thing, though. The hot water felt more than nice, it felt like the best thing ever ... until I caught sight of a fat, black spider lurking in the corner of the ceiling. It never moved, but I spent the rest of my shower too terrified to relax.

After Aunt Junie's shower we went to check on Boone. The sky spit snowflakes and I was afraid my damp hair might freeze solid. We drove around the block, out of sight of the shelter and I let Boone out to do his business and fed him dinner. I hugged my arms over my chest and shivered while he crunched his kibble. This part of the city was mostly railroad tracks, old houses and deserted lots—definitely not the part you'd advertise on a website—and the dark and cold made everything even more ugly and depressing.

"You know," Aunt Junie said, as we pulled back into the shelter parking lot, "it wouldn't really be safe for you to spend the night out here in the car."

I shivered, unwilling to admit I'd been thinking the same thing. "But we've been sleeping in the car every night."

"This isn't the Flying J, Shannon. You heard what Sue said."

"Then what about Boone? He won't be safe either."

She sighed. "The windows are tinted. No one will even know he's out here, and the car will be locked."

I gazed into Boone's eyes and felt myself faltering. I knew she was probably right, nobody would even see him . . . but still. I glanced at the building. At least our room was at this end, near the car, and we were parked only a few yards from the front door. I'd sneak down and check on him later. "Can you pop the trunk?" I asked. "I want to give him my cheetah blanket."

Aunt Junie's eyes lit up. "Sure," she said, and I knew she hadn't expected me to give in so easily. It was almost enough to make me change my mind.

I grabbed the blanket, piled it into a big nest on the front seat and plopped Boone in the middle. He wagged his stub tail and gave my finger a teasing bite like we were playing some fun new game. I kissed his head. "Be a good boy," I told him. "I'm not very far away, and I'll see you real soon."

"Yeah, be good," Aunt Junie echoed. "And be *quiet*."

As soon as we got back to the room Aunt Junie flopped across the bed and clicked on the TV. They were playing a comedy hour with Jay Leno which made me think of Mitzi since she wanted to be a stand-up comedian when she grew up. I watched it for a few minutes until I remembered the shirt and leggings from the lost and found box. Hand me downs were fine, but I wanted to wash them first. "We really need to go to a laundromat," I said.

Aunt Junie scowled at her phone. "Huh? Oh, yeah. I forgot to ask if they had washing machines here. I'll check tomorrow." She nodded toward the duffle bag she'd lugged in from the car. "Still some soap in there."

I carried the clothes and the little bottle of Dawn over to the sink. The basin was the size of a mixing bowl and had crusty yellowish gunk all around the drain. There was barely room for the shirt, much less the leggings, but I forced everything in and sloshed it around, splashing water and not caring. I thought about the woman spitting corn bread all over the table, and Boone out there by himself, and about how Aunt Junie and I did not belong in this disgusting place. I didn't realize I was clenching my teeth until I felt the ache in my jaws.

The clinking of glass made me look up, and I watched Aunt Junie pour herself a double shot of tequila. "What are you doing? Sue said you're not allowed to have…"

She hushed me with a finger to her lips. "What Sue doesn't know won't hurt her." She stared at the TV and sipped her drink. I didn't understand how she could stomach the stuff. I'd snuck a swallow once and thought my head might burst into flame.

I wrung out the shirt and leggings the best I could and looked for a place to hang them. Our wet towels were already over the back of the recliner, and there really wasn't any other good spot. I finally draped the shirt over the edge of the coffee table, and the leggings over an arm of the

58

recliner. And there was something about the whole ordeal that left me feeling exhausted. I plopped down on the cot.

"Got any homework?" Aunt Junie asked.

I shrugged. I did. I had a ton of missed work to make up, but the lighting in the room was awful, and my mind felt like a lump anyway. "A little," I said. "But I'm really tired … and hungry."

"You should've finished your dinner. There's granola bars in the duffle bag."

I huffed a sigh. I was sick to the brim of granola bars. "Know what I really want?"

Aunt Junie pursed her lips, like she was afraid it might be a trick question. "Um … no."

"A bacon cheeseburger with a pile of greasy fries on the side, and a strawberry milkshake with whipped cream on top."

She smiled. "Wow. Didn't even have to think about that, did you?"

"Actually, I've been thinking about it for weeks."

"Yeah," she said, softly.

"How 'bout you?" I asked.

"How 'bout me what?"

"If you could go to a restaurant and order anything at all, without worrying about how much it cost, what would you have?"

Her eyebrows peaked. "Hmmm, let me think. Anything at all?"

"Anything."

"Probably prime rib, and a baked potato with the works, you know, sour cream, chives, bacon bits ... and maybe some of those little asparagus spears in cream sauce."

I nodded my approval. "And for dessert?"

"Ooooh, we get dessert too? Okay, let's see ... " she tapped her chin. "Probably either lemon cheesecake or pecan pie. Why not both?"

I clutched my stomach. "Sounds soooo good."

"Yeah, well, hold that thought, okay? Because one of these days soon, when this whole mess is behind us, we'll go out and celebrate with a victory dinner to die for."

I gave a wistful sigh. "You pinkie swear?"

Aunt Junie solemnly held up her pinkie and wiggled it. "Pinkie swear," she said. Then she reached for the bottle of tequila and refilled her shot glass.

Aunt Junie fell into a deep, snoring slumber not long after we shut off the lights, but I lay staring into the darkness, feeling as if I'd downed an energy drink. Every time somebody stomped up the stairs, flushed the toilet or shut their door, I flinched. So much for no noise after ten.

It was 1:15 when I crept over to the window to check on Boone, but even with my hands cupped around my face it was too dark to see the parking lot. I rocked back and forth on my toes and tried to decide which was worse—not being sure he was okay, or going out to check and getting him all excited only to leave again? It was like being the rope in a game of tug of war.

I went back to bed and reread the information on the Silver Heart Essay. I'd been so excited at first. But now, I wondered how I'd ever convince Aunt Junie to enter. She'd probably think it was too much of a longshot to bother, a waste of time with so much bigger stuff to worry about—like a job, or food, or enough quarters to do a load of laundry. And even if she did think it was worth entering, she didn't have a computer to type on anyway.

But then after a while, an idea came to me. An idea that made my heart throb. *I* had the time, and I had an iPad at school. I could write the essay for her. We had a quiz on the Renaissance tomorrow afternoon, so if I finished early I'd have free time on the iPad. If I could figure out how to word the essay tonight, it would only take a few minutes to type tomorrow. And so what if it *was* a crazy long shot, it was still a shot. At least I'd be doing something to try and help, something to prove I wasn't useless. And if it worked... oh, if it worked.

I was revising the essay in my mind for the fourth or fifth time when a loud *"Pop-Pop-Pop"* made me bolt up. Loud laughter, swearing and the banging of car doors came from the parking lot. I raced to the window. A tiny flame flickered through the darkness, followed by the red glow of a cigarette. And then I heard it... short, muffled yapping.

Boone!

My blood turned cold. What if somebody was trying to get him?

I groped through Aunt Junie's purse for the keys before jamming my feet into my shoes and fumbling to unlock the door. I aimed the light from my phone toward my feet, dragging a hand along the wall as I fled through the dark hall and down the flight of stairs to the lobby.

I rammed into the corner of Sue's desk and sucked in a sharp breath as pain ripped through my thigh. I limped across the lobby and wrestled with the dead bolt. Even after it slid free, the door only opened a couple inches. It was stuck, but I couldn't tell on what. I jerked as hard as I could. Whatever was holding it finally gave way and an ear splitting chirping filled the air as I raced outside.

At least an inch of snow had fallen, and I slipped and slid my way to the Impala. Boone stood with his face to the window, barking for all he was worth, his little puffs of breath fogging the glass. I unlocked the driver's door and cradled him in my arms. His little body was a popsicle and I started to cry. "It's okay, boy. It's me, Boone. I've got you now."

He trembled with happiness, licking my face with a chilled tongue, and I felt like the worst pet owner in the whole world. "I'm so sorry, boy. I'm so sorry I left you out here by yourself."

A car door slammed, and I whirled around to see a squat figure in a canvas coat looming out of the darkness in front of me. "Hey, there, girlie. Now what you got there?"

I cringed away from the man's tangled beard and the stink of alcohol on his breath. "Leave me alone," I shrieked.

He put a hand on my arm. "Now that's not very friendly of ya."

Boone chomped down on his fingers and the man jerked back, cursing. I wheeled past him and ran for the building. The horrible chirping alarm was still blaring as I rushed into the lobby. A light shone from somewhere in the back and saved me from smashing into any more furniture as I made a beeline for the stairs.

I almost made it.

"Hey! Stop!"

The commanding voice was loud enough to hear over the alarm and I froze in my tracks.

Sue glared at me, her hair wild, a baseball bat clutched in her hands. She lowered the bat, strode over and shut off the alarm. "What do you think you're doing?" she bellowed.

My ears kept right on ringing. "There's this m-man outside," I stammered. "He grabbed my arm. He's in the parking lot."

"What were you doing out there? It's three in the morning."

"I heard l-l-loud noises. I thought somebody was hurting my dog. I had to go check and there was this ..."

Sue shut and relocked the door. "You broke my chain lock," she accused.

I shook my head. "What! No ... I just opened it. I didn't know there was an alarm."

"You broke it," she repeated, lifting one end of the dangling chain.

And with a sick feeling I remembered how the door refused to open even after I'd unfastened the deadbolt. Now I knew why. Goose bumps popped up all over me. "Oooooh," I breathed. "I'm ... I'm ... I didn't mean to."

"And there are NO pets allowed. I told you and your aunt that."

"I know. But I was afraid somebody was hurting him. And he was cold, too. I couldn't just leave him in the car."

"Then you should've found somewhere else for him to stay."

I swallowed. How could she not understand? How could she be such an almighty jerk? "I don't have anywhere else for him to stay."

Doors opened and heads peeked over the railing above. One woman stood there in her bra and underpants.

"Everybody go back to bed," Sue grumbled. "It's okay."

"Shannon?"

Aunt Junie wavered at the top of the stairs, her face pale, one hand braced on the banister. "What's going on?"

"She broke my lock and set off the alarm so she could sneak her dog in. That's what's going on," Sue said.

Up until right then I'd only been scared, but now my nose burned with fury. "No, it's not," I said. "There was something going on in the parking lot. There's this guy and ..."

Sue put her hands on her hips. "There are always people up to no good around here. That's why we have locks and an alarm."

I gaped at her. I couldn't believe nobody cared what had been going on out there. Nobody cared a drunk man grabbed me, that something way worse could have happened to me and Boone.

Aunt Junie looked between us. She opened her mouth but then closed it again.

"Now, I'm sorry," Sue continued, not sounding sorry at all, "but the only way we can keep any semblance of order around here is to enforce the rules. I'm not heartless enough to kick you out in the middle of the night, but you will have to leave in the morning."

Good, I wanted to shout. *I never wanted to stay at your worthless shelter anyway.* But the lost look on Aunt Junie's face filled me with overwhelming guilt, and I couldn't say anything at all.

"I understand," she said, softly.

Sue glared at me a few seconds longer before focusing on Boone. She rolled her eyes and huffed out a breath. "You can keep him with you for the few hours you have left."

I bolted up the stairs, afraid she might change her mind if I didn't disappear instantly.

Aunt Junie padded back to the room after me and relocked the door behind us.

"Did you hear all the noise outside, Aunt Junie? It was so..."

Her accusing look shut me up. "All I wanted was one decent night's sleep, Shannon. Just one. Was it so much to ask?"

It felt like she'd thrown a glass of cold water in my face. Tears raced down my cheeks and plopped onto Boone's head. "I know," I said. "I didn't mean to..."

She put her fingertips against her temples. "Stop," she hissed. "Just stop. My head's already killing me." She tottered back to the bed, dropped onto it and yanked the blankets over her head.

I stared after her, stunned. I had to spread my feet to keep my balance, sure the floor was heaving beneath me. How did I keep coming up with new reasons for Aunt Junie to hate me, when all I really wanted was for her to love me?

CHAPTER SEVEN

I TIPTOED AROUND THE room later that morning, gathering our things and doing my best to keep Boone quiet. Aunt Junie slouched on the edge of the bed with her head cradled in her hands. I handed her the shirt she pointed to, then her hairbrush, and finally a glass of water. "Why don't you drink this," I said. "Maybe it'll make you feel a little better."

She took a few sips before setting the glass on the rug and stumbling past me on the way to the bathroom. The leggings I'd washed were dry, but the T-shirt was still damp, and it took all my will power not to scream when I pulled it over my head. I sucked in my stomach, willing the material not to touch my skin, but of course it didn't work. And I knew I'd have to endure the misery for at least a couple of hours before it finished drying.

Aunt Junie dragged back a few minutes later, her hair bound in a loose ponytail and her face scrubbed. She surveyed the room with a bleak expression.

"I think I got everything," I said, careful to keep my voice low. My stomach refused to be quiet though, it growled super loud as usual.

"We can't eat here," Aunt Junie said. "But I know someplace we can get breakfast."

"Where?" I asked, so relieved to hear her voice. After the nightmare of rescuing Boone, I feared she might never talk to me again.

"The Methodist Church on Brown Street. They have free meals on Thursdays."

"Okay." I scooped Boone up in one arm and our duffle bag in the other. "Do you think it will take long? School starts in a half hour."

She picked up her purse. "Shouldn't."

A big welcome sign hung on the double doors of the Methodist church, and a couple dozen people milled around inside balancing Styrofoam cups and plates. The friendly buzz of conversation grated on me. People had no business acting happy to be at a free breakfast for the poor. They should all be just as ashamed as me. I hid behind Aunt Junie, checking out the room and praying I didn't recognize anyone.

A burly guy in a white apron presided over a steaming griddle, whistling as he poured puddles of batter on the spattering surface. "Step right up, ladies," he called to us. "Step right up and taste Big Sam's fantastic blueberry pancakes. And if you've ever tasted any better, I don't wanna hear about it." He winked as he passed me a plate.

Besides pancakes with maple syrup, there was bacon, hash browns, toast and apple juice, and it was way better than I expected a free breakfast to be. Aunt Junie and I sat on green plastic chairs near a neatly dressed lady with a little girl about two years old. The little girl had pony tails with ribbons and she studied me with big brown eyes as she noisily sucked the grease off her strip of bacon. I wondered why they were here. They didn't look poor. They definitely didn't look homeless. They looked like normal, decent people—just like most of the other people here—just like us.

But then I thought about Aunt Junie insisting that *we* were homeless, and it gave me a start to realize maybe my idea about being homeless was messed up. Maybe having a car didn't make us not homeless, maybe it just made us . . . lucky. But I didn't feel lucky. I felt like I had when I was six and I followed a squirrel into the woods before suddenly realizing I couldn't see our cabin anymore. I knew I wasn't actually lost. A dozen steps to the left would bring it back into view. Or was it a dozen steps to the right? And for a few seconds the terror of being swallowed by five thousand acres of state forest land paralyzed me. And that's how I felt right now. Maybe Aunt Junie and I weren't hopelessly lost, but just a couple more steps in the wrong direction and we would be.

Aunt Junie went back for a second cup of coffee, and I glanced at my phone. We needed to go, school started in only eight minutes and I absolutely could not be late again. But after last night, I knew better than to rock the boat.

I ended up fifteen minutes late.

All the kids gawked as I crossed to my desk, and I wanted to slap the whole lot of them. My heart shrank even more when I saw Mitzi's empty chair. I needed her to be there. I needed a friend. "Sorry," I mumbled, when Mrs. Stedman caught sight of me.

"Very glad you made it," she said, smiling. "But Mitzi just took the attendance to the office. You'll need to go and tell Officer Murphy you're here after all."

My mouth felt like it was stuffed with cotton balls. "Um ... you mean, right now?"

Levi snorted. "No, tomorrow." And everyone laughed.

A terrible burning pressure filled my nose, and I bit the inside of my cheek to keep my face straight.

Mrs. Stedman cut Levi a sharp look before nodding at me. "Yes, Shannon, right now before it gets entered in the computer. Then hurry back. I was just about to share some information about our upcoming read-a-thon."

I backed out of the room and dragged toward the office with sweaty hands. Officer Murphy would ask why I was late again. He'd ask more questions about Aunt Junie. What was I supposed to say?

Mitzi and I almost knocked heads as we rounded the corner. We both skidded to a stop and Mitzi pumped her fists. "Yay," she said. "You're here."

I forced a grin. "Yep, I thought you were gone too."

"Something happen? Is that why you're late?"

I rolled my eyes. "Naw, I'm good. Just forgot to set my alarm."

Mitzi giggled. "I do that all the time, but then Mom storms in to get me. Well, see you back in class."

I took a quick glance over my shoulder before grabbing her arm. "Wait ... Mitzi? Could you do me a really big favor?"

Her eyes widened and she leaned close. "Sure I can. What?"

I knew she meant it, and her willingness made me want to burst into tears and hug her at the same time. "Can you go back to the office and tell Officer Murphy I'm here? Mrs. Stedman sent me to do it, but can you pleeeese?"

She drew back, and I could see her brain turning cartwheels as she struggled to piece things together. "Um ... okay. Are you in trouble with him for something?"

I shook my head. "I just don't want him to ask me questions right now, okay?"

Mitzi's eyebrows hunched. "Sure. But if I do it, will you tell me what's going on at lunch?"

"Yeah," I said, but my stomach clenched, because I knew I was promising something I couldn't do.

"Cool." She wheeled back for the office, and I quickly ducked into the restroom. I peeled off my sweatshirt and pushed the button on the hand dryer. The blast of warm air felt wonderful against my still damp shirt, and I held it out and slowly twisted from side to side as I tried to decide what to tell Mitzi at lunch. I couldn't tell her about living in a car, or about getting kicked out of the homeless shelter, or about eating free breakfast at church.

I wished we were good enough friends for me to tell her the real story. But I was scared to risk such a huge secret. She might tell the other kids. Even if she didn't, it was a pretty sure bet she wouldn't want to be my friend anymore. And I needed to hold onto our friendship as long as I could.

And then it came to me. I could tell her about running into Officer Murphy at the Flying J, how he'd smelled alcohol and questioned Aunt Junie about drinking and driving. She'd think I wanted to avoid him because I was still embarrassed. At least it wouldn't be a lie.

"Good," Mrs. Stedman said, as soon as we both returned, "everyone's here. The read-a-thon starts next week boys and girls, so now's the time to start gathering sponsors. There are some terrific prizes this year. Gift certificates for Skate Plaza, Pizza Hut, and Barnes and Nobles, and the grand prize is one admission to the summer camp Parks and Rec is offering."

There were plenty of eager head bobs and "ooohhs" and "ahhhs," but their enthusiasm left me feeling like I'd sucked on a lemon. Read-a-thon's weren't any fun without sponsors, and I couldn't think of a single person to ask. Aunt Junie definitely didn't have money to sponsor me. I cut my eyes to the clock, restless for a chance to type the Silver Heart Essay for her. I'd written at least ten versions in my head—I was ready.

Finally, the clock crept around, and Mrs. Stedman asked Mitzi to pass out our iPads. I slammed through the seventeen questions on the Renaissance quiz in only twelve minutes and then quickly opened the blank form for the Silver Heart Essay. My fingers flew over the keyboard with a sense of urgency I'd never felt before.

My name is Shannon O'Reilly, and I'm twelve years old. I'm not supposed to be writing this essay, my aunt Junie is. But she doesn't have a computer, and even if she did, I think she's too discouraged to try. But that doesn't mean she doesn't deserve to win. If you could just meet her, and get to know her, then you'd see. But since you don't know her, I'm going to try and help you understand why she should win.

My aunt is thirty four years old, and my mom and I lived with her in Plummer, Idaho from the time I was born. She did hair and nails and loved her job. She almost had enough money saved to go back to school and become an esthetician. But then something awful happened. My mom

73

got breast cancer. I didn't know how to help her, I was only eight. But Aunt Junie knew what to do. She drove Mom to every doctor appointment and sat with her during each chemo treatment. She taught me to give Mom neck rubs and to put cool washcloths on her forehead to help her deal with the side effects of the drugs. She held the plastic bowl when Mom needed to throw up. She helped her to the bathroom when she was too weak to walk on her own.

There were good days too. Days when Mom felt pretty strong. That's when she'd sit on the couch with me and read books, or watch a movie. Aunt Junie would make tater-tot casserole, or spinach quiche. But Mom's favorite was cheesy broccoli soup—I even learned to make it. The three of us played a lot of Mexican train dominoes. But my favorite game was beauty shop. We played it a lot when Mom's hair started to fall out and she felt ugly. Aunt Junie used makeup and colorful scarves to make Mom feel beautiful again. She would French braid my hair too, and we would wear scarves to match Mom's.

While she was taking care of Mom, she was also working and taking care of me. She helped me with homework, signed my permission slips for field trips, and she came to my fourth grade play when Mom was too sick.

My mom has been gone for two years now, and it's been really hard. If Aunt Junie hadn't agreed to keep me, I would probably be a foster kid. But the problem is, she never planned on having to raise me. I'm the reason we couldn't afford to stay in Plummer anymore. We came to Washington because jobs pay more, but Aunt Junie can't afford to take the tests she needs to do hair and nails here. Right now she has no job and is super stressed out. Sometimes she drinks when she's tired or upset or needs help sleeping.

Now that she has me to worry about, Aunt Junie is afraid she'll never be able to work at a job she loves again. This essay is my way of trying to repay her for all she did for Mom and for me too. I would be so, so, so, grateful if you'd consider giving one of your silver heart awards to my aunt. She would make such a great esthetician because she's so good with hair and makeup, and she knows how to make people smile and feel good about themselves. She really does have a heart of silver.

Sincerely

Shannon O'Reilly

Mrs. Stedman always told us that first drafts were never good, that you should always revise to make them better. But there wasn't time. I only got to do a quick check for typos before Mrs. Stedman said, "Okay, boys and girls, times up."

I clicked *Submit*.

CHAPTER EIGHT

UNT JUNIE'S TRAIN whistle ring tone woke me the next morning. My neck was kinked from being squished against the Impala's hard plastic arm rest. I rubbed the ache and groggily looked around. Aunt Junie was sprawled across the front seat, one sock covered foot propped on the passenger headrest. Boone lay in a patch of sunshine in the back window—way too big a patch for six thirty. "Oh, no," I gasped. I groped for my phone, afraid to look.

Eight-forty!

I was already forty minutes late for school. Not again. I couldn't believe it.

Boone plopped onto my chest and started licking my face, and I pushed him off with a groan. I leaned over the front seat and shook Aunt Junie's shoulder. "Wake up, Aunt Junie. It's really late."

She jumped with a moan. "Mmmm?"

"It's going on nine o'clock," I said. "We slept through the alarm." I wiped condensation from the window to peer outside—the overnight lot was empty except for a brown mini-van and a green pick up with Florida plates.

Aunt Junie opened her eyes. They were sunken and rimmed with red, and it scared me to see them like that. Had she been drinking during the night? I'd heard the car running once, but that was about all I remembered. "We slept through the alarm," I repeated. "And you just missed a call too."

"Who from?" she asked, her words slurry.

"I dunno, I'll check." I grabbed her phone off the dash and played the voice mail. I squealed. "It's some guy named Dave from Costco, Aunt Junie. He wants you to come in for a job interview at ten o'clock."

A flicker of life came into her eyes and she struggled to sit up. "Costco? Really? Gimme the phone."

She closed her eyes and rubbed little circles on her forehead as she listened. "Oh, my God," she breathed. "Ten o'clock, that's only an hour from now. I've gotta get cleaned up." She fumbled in the glove box for her bottle of aspirin and shook three pills into her hand, washing them down with a sip from her water bottle. She blinked at me. "Oh, wait ... what about school?"

I hesitated. I really needed to be there. But I couldn't expect anybody to cover for me with Officer Murphy two days in a row. I'd have to face him. I hadn't done my homework either. Besides, if Aunt Junie had any chance of getting this job, I had to do whatever I could to help her. "I think it might be too late for me to go now," I said. "I'll help you get ready."

"Crap," she said. "Donny will be after me again."

I stared at her. "What?"

Her eyes widened a little, as if she'd been caught doing something sneaky. She flicked her hand. "Nothing. Do something with your dog, he's jumping all over."

I snapped on Boone's leash and walked him around the lot for a few minutes. Then Aunt Junie and I made our way over to the restroom and washed up the best we could. I slipped into one of the stalls to put on my last clean pair of underwear. My tie-dye shirt wasn't very clean, but it had so many colors it hid stains really well. I did my best to smooth out the wrinkles, and then tamed my hair into a half bun while Aunt Junie applied her eye liner and mascara. She squeezed a tiny dab of paste on her toothbrush. It was only a sample size tube and nearly flat, but we'd made it last since leaving Plummer. She quickly brushed and then breathed into her hands to check her breath. "Better," she said, tossing me the tube. "Here, brush. I'm sure you're overdue."

I quickly brushed while she dabbed on lipstick and rubbed her lips together to even it out. "Well," she asked, "do I look half way presentable?"

Half way was pretty accurate, but I nodded encouragingly. "You look good."

My stomach thundered as we headed back to the Impala, but Aunt Junie didn't seem to notice. "You know what's funny?" she asked. "I applied for a bunch of jobs online at the library the other day, but I don't even remember one of them being Costco."

"I know you'd rather work at a spa, but Costco would be okay, right?"

She sniffed. "Beggars can't be choosers."

The bright sunshine was a welcome change from the gray we'd had lately. It made me feel hopeful. But it didn't seem to have that effect on Aunt Junie, because as soon as we headed out of the truck stop she put on her sunglasses and flipped down the visor.

I rested my forehead against the passenger window and held tight to Boone so he wouldn't jump on Aunt Junie. "Do you remember where Costco is?" I asked, as we passed the reflective green glass of the Wells Fargo Bank.

"Mmm, pretty much." The car swerved a little as she reached to turn on the radio. "Hey," she grumbled, as static filled the air, "what happened to KZZK?"

"I didn't turn it," I said.

"What is it, 99.2?"

"Sounds right." I watched as she fumbled with the knob, turning it first one direction and then the other as she searched for her favorite rock station.

"Here," I said, "maybe you better let me—" my words were cut short by a sudden blur of gray beside me.

My arms tightened around Boone as the squeal of brakes filled the air. "Watch out! Watch out!"

Aunt Junie jerked the wheel. There was a terrible crunch and my head smacked the headrest. Boone flew from my arms and hit the floorboard with a yelp. My seatbelt locked as we came to a hard stop. For a few seconds there was only silence, then Boone jumped back onto my lap, whimpering.

Aunt Junie looked stunned. "Are you okay, Shannon?"

I looked down at myself. "Um … yeah, I'm fine."

"I never saw him," she panted. "Crap, I swear I didn't see him." The Impala sat sideways, the front half in one lane and the back sticking into the next. The blur of gray next to my window was a shiny SUV that now sat directly in front of us, its chrome bumper crumpled.

Aunt Junie crossed her arms over the steering wheel and hid her face. "Oh, no," she moaned. "Ohhhh, no."

I took a shaky breath. "It's okay," I said. "It's okay, Aunt Junie. It wasn't your fault." But I'm not sure why I said it, because I really had no idea what happened, much less whose fault it was.

The door of the SUV swung open and an older man in a suit and tie slid out. He strode over to Aunt Junie's side, his face tight with concern. He tapped on the glass and stooped to peer inside as she lowered her window. "Everybody okay?"

"We're fine," Aunt Junie managed. "What happened?"

His lip curled in disbelief. "You swerved into my lane, that's what happened. There was no way to avoid you."

Aunt Junie gulped. "I'm so sorry," she said. "I never saw you. I swear I didn't."

His steely gaze swept over me and Boone, and I got the feeling he was trying to be nice because there was a kid in the car. He pulled out his phone. "Well, you've got insurance, I hope."

"Oh … sure," Aunt Junie said. "Of course."

"All right. I'm gonna call and report it."

I focused on the slicked back hair covering his bald spot as he called the police and gave brief details. "Someone will be here in a minute," he said. "Then we can exchange information." He went back to his car.

Aunt Junie's face was the color of copy paper and it scared me silly. "What's gonna happen when the cops come?" I asked. "I've never been in an accident."

"It won't be good," she said. "Not good."

Panic swelled my insides like air in an inner tube. "What won't be good, Aunt Junie? What's going to happen?"

"They'll write a report," she said. "Take pictures of the damage. Try and determine whose fault it is."

"I don't think our car has any damage," I said. "At least it doesn't look like it from in here. Will you get a ticket if they think it's your fault?"

She bit her bottom lip and blinked super-fast. "I'm so sorry, bug. So sorry you got stuck with a loser like me."

Her words were like a nail in my stomach, twisting and tearing. "I told you, you're not a loser. Quit saying stuff like that."

"But this whole mess," she spread her hands wide, and I knew she was talking about a lot more than just the accident.

"We'll get through it," I said, "we have so far."

Two patrol cars showed up. An officer in a bright green safety vest started directing traffic. Another headed for the driver of the SUV, and a third came up to Aunt Junie's side of the car. He had a bushy black moustache and a no-nonsense expression. "You folks all right?" he asked. "Anybody hurt?"

"We're fine," Aunt Junie said, her voice quiet. "Just a little shook up is all."

That was an understatement. My hands were practically jumping. I hid them in Boone's fur. His little ears were peaked and he was trembling too. "I'm good," I said.

He nodded. "Can you tell me what happened?"

Aunt Junie made a limp gesture toward the SUV. "I'm not really sure, officer. He says I swerved into his lane."

The officer's gaze bored into Aunt Junie's face. "Your eyes are awfully red, ma'am. Have you been drinking?"

"No sir. I mean … not recently."

"What's not recently mean?"

"Last night … it's been several hours."

"Uh, huh," he said, like he'd heard the same line a million times. "And what did you drink?"

"Tequila."

"How much?"

Aunt Junie curled her hands. "I'm not sure," she said. "Not much ... a few shots."

She wasn't looking at the cop's face, but I was. And I suddenly got it. I understood why Aunt Junie was so anxious. It wasn't the accident, or fear of a ticket. It was the fact that she'd been drinking. A big bulge of fear clogged my throat and made it hard to swallow.

"Is this your daughter?" he asked, tipping his head toward me.

"My niece, Shannon," Aunt Junie said. "She lives with me."

Right here in the car, I almost added.

The police officer sighed. "All right, ma'am, let's start with your license and proof of insurance, please."

Aunt Junie fumbled through her purse. "I'm afraid I don't have insurance right now. I did ... until just recently. But I didn't have the money to renew my policy." She handed over her license with shaking fingers. "We're new here, and I'm not working yet and ..." her voice trailed off and she dropped her gaze.

The officer studied her license. "Have you ever been cited for DUI before?"

Her shoulders wilted.

"Be honest," he said, "because as soon as I run your license I'll know anyway."

"Twice," she said, softly.

I'm not sure if my mouth actually dropped open or if it just felt like it did. Only a few days ago she'd told Officer Murphy she'd never drink and drive, that she wasn't that stupid. But now she was admitting she'd been caught doing that very thing ... *twice*.

"Will you voluntarily agree to a field sobriety test?"

Aunt Junie's throat bobbed as she swallowed. "Yes, sir."

The officer glanced over at me and Boone. He didn't exactly smile, but his cheeks relaxed like maybe he wanted to. Like I said, it's pretty hard to look at Boone and not smile. "Let's have you all move over to the sidewalk where it's safer. I'll run your license and be right there in a minute."

We crossed the street, and I backed up against the brick wall of Featherstone's Appliance. Cold sweat tickled my underarms and made me shiver. I watched the cop in the green vest direct traffic, impatiently motioning to drivers who crawled by with necks craned, as if they'd never seen a crumpled bumper before.

Aunt Junie stood beside me, her head low and her shoulders hunched like a turtle hiding in its shell. My teeth chattered. "What's gonna happen, Aunt Junie?"

"I'm not sure," she mumbled. And those three words made me feel like she'd pushed me off a ledge in the dark.

And there's nothing scarier than falling and not knowing where you're going to land.

The officer came over a few minutes later and motioned Aunt Junie further down the sidewalk. The traffic noise blocked his voice as he demonstrated a series of heel to toe steps. Then he wiggled his finger at Aunt Junie.

She took slow, cautious steps toward him, her arms at her sides, swaying slightly, stepping out to the side once. Next, the officer placed his heels together and raised his right leg about six inches off the ground, holding it there for what seemed like a long time. I held my breath as Aunt Junie carefully raised her foot, but started to topple right away. She took a quick hop to catch herself. He gave her another chance, but she couldn't do it that time either. Then he pulled a pen from his chest pocket and held it close to her face, slowly moving it from side to side.

I forgot I was holding my breath until black shadows swam before my eyes, and I squatted down against the building to keep from dropping Boone. When I looked again, Aunt Junie was blowing into a skinny glass tube. I knew it was a breathalyzer. Officer Murphy had shown us one during a school assembly not long ago. It measured a person's blood alcohol level, and as I watched her now, hot shame burned through my veins until I had to turn away. And I wished Boone and I were somewhere far away, with anyone else.

The officer and Aunt Junie talked for several more minutes, then they both looked toward me, and my whole body stiffened. I scrambled to my feet as the officer pulled handcuffs from his belt and snapped them on Aunt Junie.

"No," I cried, jogging the last few feet. "What are you doing? What's happening, Aunt Junie?"

She dropped her head close to mine. "It's okay, bug. It's gonna be okay. I failed my sobriety test."

"Failed your . . . what does that even mean?" I demanded. "What are they gonna do?"

The officer adjusted his cap. "Your aunt's being arrested for driving under the influence of alcohol," he explained in a gentle voice. "She'll need to come with us down to the police station."

I shook all over. "But what about me and Boone, Aunt Junie? You can't leave us."

"I'm not leaving you. You can come with me."

"But then what? What's gonna happen after that?"

She gave me a defeated look. "I'm so sorry, Shannon. Believe me, I am."

But I didn't believe her. I couldn't believe any of it. As if enough bad stuff hadn't happened already, and now Aunt Junie was under arrest for DUI? Wouldn't that completely wipe out her chances of being awarded one of the Silver Heart Essay scholarships? Why in the world couldn't I just have a normal life like every other twelve year old kid?

CHAPTER NINE

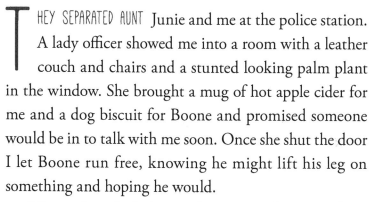

THEY SEPARATED AUNT Junie and me at the police station. A lady officer showed me into a room with a leather couch and chairs and a stunted looking palm plant in the window. She brought a mug of hot apple cider for me and a dog biscuit for Boone and promised someone would be in to talk with me soon. Once she shut the door I let Boone run free, knowing he might lift his leg on something and hoping he would.

I listened to the light grinding noise of a copier from some nearby room and felt sorry for the palm. Its leaves were curled on the tips and there were yellow patchy parts on most of them. I thought how much bigger and happier it would be if it lived where it actually belonged—someplace tropical with lots of fresh air and sun and warm ocean breezes—instead of suffocating in this stupid room with stuffy, fake heat, and I knew just how it felt. What I didn't know was what to do next.

My cider was long gone before I heard the *clip-clip* of footsteps approaching and a woman stepped into the room. She wore a silky T-shirt over a calf-length skirt and sandals. Boone yipped at her, and she pulled back with a startled laugh. "Well, well, hello to you too little fella. What is your name?"

"Boone," I said.

His ears pricked up at the sound of his name and he turned into a wiggling worm of happiness. "Awww," the lady said. She offered me her hand. "You must be Shannon. I'm Rebecca Kinney. I'm a social worker, and I'm here to help you."

My senses jumped to full alert. "A social worker? Do you put kids in foster care?"

Boone rolled onto his back and the lady squatted down to rub his tummy. "Finding safe homes for children in need is definitely part of my job. What makes you ask?"

I swallowed. "I used to have a friend ... a best friend. She got taken away from her family and put into a foster home when we were eight. And I've never seen her since."

Miss Kinney plucked a thread from her shirt. "I just met you, but I can already tell you'd make a very good friend." She scooted a chair over and sat with her knees almost touching mine. "One of our highest priorities in any foster care situation is to get the family back together as soon as we can. And in most cases we're able to do that. But unfortunately, there are times where it's not safe for the child to go back with their family. In those cases we try to find a long term placement, but sometimes it's not in the same town, or even in the same county. Maybe something similar happened with your friend."

What she said made sense, but it still left me with a sick feeling in my stomach and I didn't want to talk about Amber anymore. "Do you know if my aunt's okay?"

"Yes, I was just talking with her. She's fine, other than being worried about you, of course."

"Can I see her pretty soon?"

Miss Kinney cleared her throat. "You know your aunt was arrested for driving while under the influence of alcohol, right? And you probably realize that's pretty serious."

I nodded.

"Does she drink often?"

I felt a tug of loyalty for Aunt Junie. "I dunno. Sometimes."

"Okay," Miss Kinney said. "Well, here's what will happen next. First, she'll have to make an appearance in court, which won't happen until tomorrow morning. Then if she's convicted, and it's very likely she will be based on the results of her breathalyzer, she'll have to pay a fine, and she'll lose her license for a while. And unfortunately..." she paused for a moment, like she was giving me a chance to brace for something worse. "Since your aunt admitted this is not a first offense, she may be required to serve some jail time. And she'll also have to complete a mandatory alcohol education course."

I was stunned. "Jail?" I whispered, and for once my voice betrayed me. "But … it was only a dented bumper. Nobody even got hurt."

Miss Kinney raised her eyebrows. "Thank goodness," she said, "this time. But countless people are injured or even killed by—"

"I already know that," I interrupted. "But Aunt Junie wasn't drunk."

"Maybe not. But the fact that she chose to drive in her condition, especially with you in the car, proves that she has a drinking problem."

I gritted my teeth. She was wrong. Aunt Junie's only problems were no job and no home and me, of course. But I didn't say that because I wasn't sure how much Miss Kinney knew. "What's gonna happen to me?"

"I'm going to take you to meet a wonderful lady. Her name is Trina and she lives right here in Logan. You can stay with her for a bit until your aunt gets things worked out, all right?"

My heart tripled its speed. Who was this lady, and where did she live? Did she like dogs? Did she have a fenced yard? "Does she know about me?" I asked.

Miss Kinney nodded. "She does, and she's more than happy to have you."

"Did you tell her I have a dog?"

She hesitated a heartbeat, and her eyes flickered with sympathy. "We'll have to come up with some other arrangements for Boone, Shannon. Trina's not set up for pets."

A jolt of panic electrified my whole body. "No," I said. "No." I scooped Boone up and held him against my chest. "He's not going any place without me."

Miss Kinney raised her hands in surrender. "I totally understand," she said. "And I promise no one is trying to take your dog away from you. We run into this situation all the time and we're set up to handle it."

"Handle it how?" I asked.

"The humane society runs a foster care program for pets much like the one we run for children. They temporarily board pets free of charge until the owners can pick them up again. My friend Helen runs the program, and she just adores dogs."

My eyelids burned and I closed my eyes to keep the tears back. It was like being at the women's shelter all over again—only way worse. Because this time Boone wouldn't be a few yards away out in the car, he'd be gone. "I've had him since he was three months old," I said. "He wouldn't know what to do without me."

Miss Kinney smoothed her hand over Boone's head. "But he's such a friendly little guy," she said, winking. "Bet he'd be just fine for a few days. I'll ask Helen to come by so you can meet her, okay?" She pulled out her cell phone.

I wanted to jump and scream. I wanted to kick her. I wanted to grab her cell phone and hurl it across the room. But my gut told me none of it would do a bit of good, because she was using that fake, happy voice adults use when they hope you'll go along with something they've already decided to do anyway.

Helen Thomas was a tall woman with too much blush on her cheeks and a wide smile. "Well, what do we have here?" she asked, as she bustled up to the couch where I sat holding Boone. She dropped to her knees and let him sniff the back of her hand. "You've gotta be the cutest Jack Russell I've ever seen."

I wanted Boone to bite her fingers off, but of course he licked them instead. "His name is Boone," I said, my voice tight. "And he's the best dog in the world."

"I don't doubt that a bit. And what is your name, honey?"

"Shannon. Where is the humane society at?"

"On Ripley Avenue. Down by the water front, near the big salvage yard."

I tried to calm myself down enough to think. Aunt Junie and I had driven past the river front a few times. I remembered row after row of empty docks and the frame of a Ferris wheel, its seats removed for the winter. "Near the Ferris wheel?"

Helen bobbed her head. "That's it. Only a block from there."

"He needs to be inside," I said. "He's not an outside dog."

"Absolutely. All our dogs are kenneled indoors except for the big ones that clearly prefer to be outside."

"He's afraid of big dogs," I added. "Little ones are usually okay."

"Is he up to date on his shots?"

"He had the first ones when we adopted him."

"Okay, well, the only dogs we allow to socialize are those that are current on their vaccinations. So it would probably be best to keep him in his own space. Can I hold him a minute?"

I numbly let her take Boone from my arms. She nestled him close and let him lick her cheek, and it made me feel worse because I didn't want him to like her. "Will it cost anything to get him back?" I asked.

"No, honey. Donations are always welcome. But we board pets for up to a week free of charge."

A week? There was no way I was staying away from Boone for any week. "He won't be there near that long," I said. And I caught the fleeting look that passed between Miss Kinney and Helen. "He won't," I snapped, and my tears spilled over despite my very best efforts.

Boone instantly tensed and tried to climb out of Helen's arms, and she set him back in my lap. "Now you listen to me, Shannon. I love dogs, that's why I have the job I do. I promise he'll be just fine. In fact," she pulled a business card from her shirt pocket, "this is for you. It's the number to the shelter and my cell phone as well. I don't hand that out to just anybody. But you can call me and check on your little guy whenever you need to. Okay?"

I swallowed and curled my fingers around the card. I didn't trust myself to speak.

Helen took a paper from the folder she carried. "Let's get contact information for both you and your aunt, and then I'll have you sign here at the bottom. It just says you're voluntarily surrendering him to us."

I bristled. "It's not voluntary."

Helen winced. "I didn't mean it like that, honey. It's just legalese. Don't worry."

I gave her both phone numbers and scrawled my name with trembling fingers.

"Very good," Helen said, placing the paper back in the folder. Then she tipped her head and smiled at me. I lowered my eyes. Nobody spoke. There was nothing but terrible, awful silence.

I held Boone up to my face. He met my eyes and flattened his ears, and a sliver of pink edged out between his lips. I wasn't sure I'd survive it. I wanted to bolt out the door with him. But where would I go? What would I do? I dropped my head against his warm little body and inhaled as deeply as I could so I wouldn't forget his smell. Then I handed him to Helen and closed my eyes because I couldn't bear to see him looking back at me. I didn't open them again until I heard the door close.

CHAPTER TEN

FIFTEEN MINUTES LATER I sat limp in the front seat of Miss Kinney's car as we made our way across town. Low clouds had replaced the sun and it looked like it might snow.

Trina McPherson lived on the corner of 53rd and Palmer, in a small street level house with stenciled ivy crawling up both sides of the bright red door. There was no fence, but she did have a small yard. I felt a flicker of hope. Maybe if I kept Boone on his leash it would be okay. I gripped my backpack and followed Miss Kinney up the narrow strip of sidewalk.

The smell of cinnamon and ginger floated out as the door opened. An older lady greeted us, wearing a flour-dusted apron and an eager look. She bunched up her broad shoulders when she saw us. "Oh, yes, welcome you two, come in, come in."

Despite the baking mess, the kitchen looked clean with its blue granite countertops and gleaming pots and pans dangling from a silver rack mounted to the ceiling. A girl was curled up in a recliner in the living room reading a book, and seeing her gave me a start. It had never occurred to me there might be other kids.

"It's so nice to meet you, Shannon," the lady said, pumping my hand. "I'm Katrina McPherson. But please call me Trina. And over there," she pointed toward the girl in the recliner, "we have Megan James."

The girl swept black bangs from her face and raised her hand in a friendly-enough wave. "Hey."

"Hey," I said.

Trina peered over her shoulder. "And somewhere… Todd, dear, where are you? Come meet our new guest."

Thundering footsteps filled the air, and a young boy slid across the tile in his socks. If I hadn't jumped back he would've crashed smack into me.

The boy skidded to a stop and squinted at me through thick lenses that made his blue eyes look giant. "Hi. I'm nine years old, and I have OCD. Have you ever heard of it? Bet you haven't. Bet you don't have any idea what it is, 'cause most people don't know what it is, and you're probably like most people."

All I could do was stare at him. The kid was so far out there his planet hadn't even been identified.

Trina patted his shoulder. "Whoa now, buddy, take it easy. Remember how we talked about just starting with hello?"

Todd shoved his glasses up his nose. "Oh, yeah." He grinned at me. "Hello."

"Excellent," Trina praised. "Now say, 'My name is Todd. May I ask your name?'"

"Shannon O'Reilly," I said, quickly, before he could echo her words.

Trina looked thrilled. "See it works." She glanced over at the girl. "Megan, honey, would you show Shannon where to put her things?"

Megan closed her book and stood. "Yeah, sure." She gestured with her index finger. "Come on, this way."

I followed, glad to escape Todd's gawking. Megan led me into a big bedroom divided down the middle by a sheer green curtain, each side with its own twin bed and dresser. She jerked her thumb to the nearest bed, strewn with stuffed animals, video games and colored pencils. "You can probably tell this is my side. That's yours over there. Trina hung the curtain so we could have privacy." She shrugged with a smile. "Guess she didn't notice you can see right through it. She tends to be a little clueless sometimes."

I looked through the curtain and felt like throwing up. This was not my room. That was not my bed. I didn't want to be here. Was Miss Kinney actually going to leave me?

"You can have part of the closet too," Megan said. "I don't have very many clothes." She eyed my backpack. "From the looks of it, you don't either."

"I won't need many," I said. "I won't be here long."

"Okay, well, it's there if you want it."

"How long have you been here?" I asked.

"Three months."

Three months? My knees turned to pudding. "How come so long?"

Megan made a sweeping motion with her hand, as if she were brushing a bug off her pants. "Because my mom's husband hates kids, and my mom cares more about his opinion than mine."

Heat flooded my cheeks. "Oh," I said, stunned she'd pop off and admit something so sad and humiliating to a stranger. I'd never told a single soul about my dad, how he was so determined not to have a kid he'd abandoned Mom because of it. "So ... when will you get to go home?"

She snorted. "I don't wanna go home. I wanna stay right here with Trina. It's way better."

I didn't know what to say.

"How 'bout you?" Megan asked. "Why are you here?"

I paused. Miss Kinney must have told Trina what was going on. But maybe she hadn't told Megan. "Because I live with my aunt, and she had to go ... to the hospital for a couple days or so, and then I'm going home."

"You live with your aunt?"

"Yeah. My mom died a couple years ago." I grabbed my back pack and carried it over to the bed, praying it would end the questions. But when I peeked over my shoulder a minute later Megan was still there. I felt dizzy. "So what's with the other kid?" I asked. "He's pretty weird."

Megan sat on the edge of her bed and rearranged her pile of stuffed animals. "Todd? He's super smart actually."

"Is he really obsessive compulsive?"

Her head jerked back. "You know about OCD?"

"Well, not a lot. But I like reading about different conditions and stuff. I'm gonna be a doctor when I grow up."

"Oh, cool." She puffed out a breath. "Well, yeah, he really has it. Plus an autism disorder too."

"Nice," I said, and then immediately realized it made me sound like a jerk. But I didn't know how to take it back. I dumped my backpack onto the chenille bedspread so my hands had something to do.

"He's got some challenges," Megan said, softly. "But he's a really nice kid. Trina homeschools him, and it's helped him a lot."

"How long has he been here?"

"A while now." She picked up a stuffed lamb and adjusted the pink ribbon around its wooly neck. "Want her?"

"What?"

"The lamb? She's pretty cute, huh?"

"No, I'm good. But thanks."

She stared at me for a few heartbeats. Then she patted the lamb's head, as if she was afraid it might feel rejected. I just wanted her to leave. I wanted to be alone. I gestured to the things I'd dumped on the bed. "Well, I'm just gonna try and decide where to put some of this stuff... if you don't mind."

She raised a shoulder and let it drop. "Don't let me stop you," she said, and scooted from the room.

Now she probably thought I was an even bigger jerk, but I didn't have enough energy to care. I slapped my hands against my thighs and flopped back across the bed. The mattress was hard, and I had to bunch the pillow in half before it felt thick enough. The ceiling was bright white, and the walls were covered in soft blue paint in an odd swirly pattern, like it had been painted by some super energized person who couldn't control his brush. Maybe Todd had painted them.

My eyes burned and I pinched the bridge of my nose. It seemed like a month since Aunt Junie and I had left the Flying J that morning. I should be there now, with her and Boone, not here at some stranger's house. It wasn't right. Nothing was right about this whole insane situation.

"Shannon?"

I opened my eyes. Miss Kinney stood at the bedroom door. "Are you okay?"

I couldn't imagine what she expected me to say. *Yeah, super-duper. Never been better. Thanks for asking.*

She raised her eyebrows as she stepped over to me. "I know this is very challenging for you. But I promise, there are far worse places to be than here with Trina, so please try to be cooperative." She laid a business card beside me. "Try to have a good weekend, and call me if you need anything at all. I'll check with you Sunday evening unless something comes up in the meantime, all right?"

My heart sank. She was really gonna do it. She was going to leave me here. I gritted my teeth extra hard.

Miss Kinney touched my shoulder. "Okay, then. Hang in there."

I counted the seconds from the time she left the room until I heard the front door open. One-thousand-eleven. Such a crazy short time. Then the door shut, and there was something so final and terrifying about that sound, proof I'd stepped left when I should've stepped right and lost any chance of finding my way home again. And my insides loosened, like I was literally falling apart. I'd read in a medical book that when you felt out of control the best thing to do was control your breathing, so I tried it now. Deep breath in. Deep breath out. Deep breath in. Deep breath out.

I was so focused that the light tapping on the door was enough to make me jump. Trina stuck her head in the room and regarded me with a nervous look. "You okay?"

Was that the only question adults knew how to ask? "Uh, huh."

"Well, I'm not. I've got twenty four naked gingerbread men in my kitchen. Can you help?"

I blinked. Maybe it was her phony nervous look, or maybe it was the way she emphasized the word *naked*, but I couldn't help but smirk. It was exactly the sort of screwball thing Mitzi would say. "I'm not hungry."

"Well, you don't have to eat one. I just need help clothing them. Please."

I knew it was only a trick to get me out of the bedroom, to get me involved in something I didn't want to be involved in. But my comment about not being hungry was a total lie, and the sweet, warm smell of gingerbread was almost painful. Besides, if there was any hope of convincing her to let me bring Boone here, I figured I better play nice.

I followed Trina to the kitchen. The table was covered with the naked ginger bread men, bowls of frosting, and shakers full of sprinkles, mini chips and other tiny candies. Todd kneeled on a chair, lining up rows of Red Hots, his tongue pushed up inside his cheek. Megan sat next to him, shirt sleeves rolled up to her elbows. She glanced at me but didn't say anything. Who could blame her? *I'm not a jerk*, I wanted to say. *I'm actually a really nice person.*

Trina patted the back of a wooden chair across from Megan. "Sit right here and let your creativity fly. If you don't like how your cookie turns out, just eat it."

Todd studied me. "What's your favorite color, Shannon O'Reilly?"

"Um ... blue, I guess."

"Green," he said. "Is it four yet?"

Was I supposed to respond to that? I gave Trina a questioning look.

She smiled. "No, Todd. Not yet." She placed a gingerbread man on a piece of waxed paper in front of me and scooted over a bowl of blue frosting. "There you go. Have at it."

I stared at my cookie and fidgeted. I'd baked cookies with mom forever ago, but I couldn't remember ever decorating any. I watched Todd fool around with his Red Hots, and that's when I noticed everything around him was lined up. Three gingerbread men lay in front of him, their elbows touching. He had given each one four green frosting buttons, and two green stripes across each foot that might have been shoelaces. Two butter knives lay upright beside him, one on each side of his cookies, like a protective fence. His Red Hots were in rows of six, six to a row. "Is it four yet?" he asked.

"Nope," Trina said. "Remember to listen for the clock. It makes four chimes when it's four."

"What happens at four?" I asked, intrigued.

"He goes to bed," Trina said.

"Tea at three," Todd said in a sing-songy voice. "Naps at four, tea at three."

My expression must have been pretty funny because Megan giggled. "Just for a little while," she explained. "He just loves the routine of it. Go ahead, Todd, tell Shannon about your schedule."

Todd nudged another candy into place. "Tea at three, naps at four, dinner at six, showers at seven, bed at eight."

"You skipped five," I said. "What happens at five?"

"Nothing," Trina said. "He's always ignored five for some reason, haven't you buddy?"

Todd caught me staring and gave me a firm look. "Shannon O'Reilly," he said. "Decorate your cookie."

I smirked. It was too odd not to. "Yes, sir," I said. I grabbed a butter knife and slathered my gingerbread man with a light layer of blue frosting before recklessly dousing it with rainbow sprinkles. It looked like the creation of a kindergartner, and heat flashed up my neck. I grabbed another cookie, determined to give this one a little more thought. Before I knew it, I'd created a miniature Aunt Junie, with eyes of blue, a bathrobe of green, and thin streaks of yellow for hair.

The clock in the living room suddenly chimed. Todd's head flew up and he counted out loud. "One, two, three, four." He looked at Trina. "That's it. It's four o'clock."

Trina straightened from loading the dishwasher. "You are correct," she said.

Todd carefully added two more butter knives as a top and bottom fence around his gingerbread men. Then he hopped off his chair and trotted down the hall.

"Don't forget to use the bathroom," Trina called after him.

I shook my head, mystified. "So what happens if you move one of his candies out of order?"

Megan groaned. "World War Three. Please don't."

Trina latched the dishwasher and came to sit with us. "Todd's very intelligent, he just needs an orderly, routine schedule with no surprises to function best."

"Why is he with you?" I asked.

Trina lifted one of the gingerbread men and regarded it thoughtfully. "Let's just say, his parents weren't able to meet his needs." She bit the head off the cookie and flashed an evil grin. "Takes a pretty morbid person to bite off someone's head, wouldn't you agree?"

Megan giggled and bit the head off one of her creations. She looked at me. "Well, what are you waiting for?"

But I couldn't do it. I couldn't bite off Aunt Junie's head. I wished I'd made a Sue Moore cookie instead.

"We're happy to have you with us, Shannon," Trina said. "Anything special you'd like us to know about you?"

All my muscles tensed. I nibbled on the rainbow sprinkle cookie to stall for time. "Not really. I'm twelve, and I like school, and I have a little Jack Russell terrier named Boone."

Megan perked up. "You have a dog?"

"Yeah," I said, "wanna see?" I opened a picture on my phone and held it out.

Trina laughed. "Love the eye patch. What a sweetie."

"He's sooooo cute," Megan gushed. She gave a wistful smile. "I wish we could have a dog. But Todd's like, seriously allergic."

My heart squeezed. "He is?"

Trina made a face. "Yeah, poor kid. Pet dander gives him all the classic symptoms times seven—runny eyes, clogged nose, all that."

I bit the head off my rainbow cookie.

I went to bed early that night, and when Megan came in I pretended to be asleep. But the house was way too quiet, and my thoughts way too loud. A halogen light from the neighbor's garage shined directly into the bedroom window, and there was something oddly comforting about bright lights at night—until it suddenly blinked off and left me in complete darkness.

I was heartsick that my only hope of bringing Boone to Trina's was gone, and I ached for him with every ounce of me. I could smell his doggy scent and hear the "click, click, click" of his toenails across the oak floor in our cabin, and I wanted to hold him so bad my stomach hurt.

I pictured him curled into a ball in a cold, metal kennel, lonely and confused, wondering where I was and why I didn't come get him. I wasn't sure if a dog's brain worked the same as a person's, but I prayed he didn't think I'd abandoned him, that I didn't want him anymore. Because I knew that feeling. It was like stumbling around with a boulder strapped to your back. Tears squeezed out between my closed lashes. I balled the blanket in my fists and held it against my face to muffle my sniffling.

"It's okay," Megan whispered, "I cried my first night here too."

I quit breathing for a few seconds as shame oozed through me. At least the darkness hid my face. In fact, there was something deceiving about the darkness, something that made it feel almost safe. Like maybe I could say what I really needed to and nobody would remember it come morning. And for just an instant I was tempted to blurt it all out. To admit how angry I was at Mom for dying, at my dad for not loving me enough to even meet me, and at Aunt Junie for not knowing how to get us out of the mess we were in. But in the end, the darkness wasn't quite safe enough and I couldn't do it. I cleared my throat. "Um ... do you still have that lamb?"

"Oh, sure," Megan said. "Hang on." The mattress groaned as she moved and I could picture her searching. "Okay, I'm gonna toss her ... ready?"

I couldn't see anything in the blackness, but I held out my hands, and the lamb grazed my fingertips before landing with a gentle "whomp" near my stomach. "Thanks," I said. "Good night."

"G'night."

I held the lamb against my face, comforted by the feel of its soft, curly wool. Then I stuffed it down behind my knees where Boone liked to sleep and curled my legs around it.

CHAPTER ELEVEN

TODD WOKE ME the next morning, sliding back and forth across the kitchen tile in his blue Spiderman pajamas, until Trina finally told him to stop. I felt a little greedy as I gorged on bacon and eggs and French toast with homemade peach jam. I hoped Boone had gotten his breakfast. I would call Helen and make sure.

Aunt Junie would go to court today ... and maybe jail. What did they feed a person in jail? I pictured prisoners dressed in black, sitting at long metal tables, spooning up thick, gloppy oatmeal.

"Check out the gorgeous, snowy morning," Trina said, interrupting my thoughts.

Megan carried her plate to the sink. "It snowed? Cool."

I trailed her to the living room window. At least six inches had fallen, leaving everything with a thick, fluffy layer of vanilla frosting. It was deep enough to reach Boone's chest, and I pictured his eyes dancing with adventure as he plowed his way through.

"Anyone up for building a snowman?" Trina asked.

"Sure," Megan said.

"A fort," Todd said, his lips dusty with powdered sugar.

Trina shrugged. "Or a fort."

I clenched my hands. I *did* want to build a snowman, but I wanted to do it in my backyard in Plummer, not here. "I can't," I said. "I don't have my boots or gloves or anything."

"Oh, never fear," Trina said. She waltzed over to a hall closet and tugged out a plastic tote full of winter gear. "I always keep extras on hand."

Somehow that didn't surprise me. I'd need a better excuse. "Well…maybe in a while," I said. "I need to make a phone call first."

"Okie-dokie," she said, all chipper like, and I wondered if she ever got upset or mad about anything. I slipped into the privacy of the bedroom to call Helen at the humane society, pausing to read two new texts from Mitzi.

Hey, where u been? I'm worried.
R U okay? Text me. Miss U

I rubbed my forehead, disgusted with myself. Poor Mitzi. I was such a lame friend. I spent a few minutes trying to think up some kind of reply, but what was I supposed to say?

I'm ok. Be in touch soon. Miss U 2

I punched in Helen's number.

"Well, good morning, Shannon," she said. "I figured I'd be hearing from you soon."

"Is Boone okay?" I asked. "Did he get breakfast? I usually give him a handful of kibble when I get up."

"He's just fine," she said. "And yes, he had breakfast. Two small Milk Bones, which he thought were divine."

I scowled at the swirly pattern on the wall. He was not supposed to have dog biscuits, he was supposed to have kibble. "Okay ... well, I'm gonna get him just as soon as I can."

"Have you talked with your aunt yet?"

"Not yet. Later today, I hope."

"Very good. Keep me posted, all right?"

"I will," I promised. "And thank you ... for taking care of Boone."

I slipped my phone back in my pocket and looked out at the dazzling snow. Trina was dressed positively goofy in an orange ski jacket and a bright red joker hat. But she looked like she was having a good time as she and Todd formed up a knee high ridge of snow. Megan kneeled on the other side of the yard, rounding the edges off a square chunk of snow. I decided to go outside too. I had to do something to keep myself from going crazy while I waited to hear from Aunt Junie. I rummaged through Trina's plastic bin and found some boots and a pair of mittens with sheepskin lining.

I stepped outside and squinted into the incredibly clean whiteness. A black UPS truck rumbled past, one of the few things in the world that wasn't white. Todd caught sight of me and waved a gloved hand. "Want to help? We're building the world's best fortress."

"Looks like it," I said. "But you already have two people so I better help Megan."

"Good thinking," he said.

I stepped toward Megan with a hesitant look, not sure she'd want my help. But she gave a shrug and said, "You can work on the middle ball if you want."

I scooped up a mound of snow and squished it between my hands. Heavy and wet. Perfect packing snow. I dropped down on my knees to roll my snowball, patting down each new layer while I studied Trina and Todd out of the corner of my eye. Todd worked with such precision, packing a block mold to carefully stamp out each brick of snow, then trimming any excess with a plastic knife before placing it in perfect alignment with the last brick. I could see him growing up to be an architect or engineer.

"So who came here first?" I asked Megan. "You or Todd?"

She didn't look up, and for a minute I thought maybe she hadn't heard me. But then she said, "We came at the same time."

"Really? You mean like on the very same day?"

She straightened her back and rolled her shoulders in a stretch. "Todd's my brother."

I blinked. "No way. Why didn't you say that before?"

"You didn't ask."

"But we were talking about him last night and you never said anything about him being your brother."

"Well, he is. He's the whole reason we're here."

"I thought you were here because your step dad doesn't like kids."

"Not my step dad," she corrected, with an impatient flick of her wrist. "My mom's husband."

"Oh. Sorry."

"His name's Mel, but it should be moron. I have no idea what Mom sees in him. He hates both of us, thinks kids are a big pain in the butt, especially kids like Todd." She dropped her voice to a whisper. "Called him stupid and retard and anything else he could think of. He had Mom convinced to send him away to this boarding school for the mentally handicapped ... in Nevada of all places."

She said *Nevada* as if it were the moon. I waited for the rest of the story. "Which obviously didn't happen," I finally nudged.

"Nope." She puffed out a breath, and it curled in the frosty air. "But only because I didn't let it. I told the school counselor everything. What was going on at home, how Mel treated us, and how he was gonna send Todd away."

"You talked to the counselor on your own? What did she do?"

"Reported it to Child Services."

I sucked in a breath. "But didn't you know what could happen? I mean, did you realize you'd get taken away from your mom?"

"I didn't *know* anything. But what I *thought* was, it would be like a wakeup call to my mom, you know? I thought if it came right down to it, she'd pick her kids over some guy she'd only been with for six months. Wouldn't you expect any normal mother to do that?" Her throat bobbed out as she swallowed. "Never assume."

Ouch, I thought. But I didn't say it out loud. "Geez, Megan. I'm ... sorry."

She surprised me with a smile. "Thanks. But I'm not, not really anyway. Trina's great, and things are so much better here than they were at home."

"Do you still see your mom?"

"Yeah, she comes a couple times a month, and we text."

"Do you think you and Todd will ever get back with her?"

She curled her lip. "Not unless Moron disappears. But you know, I kind of expect he will since Mom's like his third wife or something."

I gently smoothed my palms over the snow ball. "You're really brave," I said.

She sniffed. "I had to do something. I mean, if it was only me, I would've just toughed it out. I could've run away or something if it got too bad. But I have to watch out for Todd. He needs some extra help, ya' know." She gazed across the yard at her brother. "Besides, family should stick together."

"Yeah," I said, softly, "they should."

The snow soaked through my jeans, numbing my knees, and I rocked back on my heels and thought about Megan's story. The two of us had some things in common. We'd both lost our moms. Me for real, and Megan in a different sort of way. And both of us knew what it was like to feel unwanted, to feel like a burden. But that's where the similarities ended. Because Megan had been brave enough to get help, to risk confiding in someone about what was happening with her family. But me? I was so scared of people finding out the truth and thinking badly about us, I'd allowed my life to become a big, fat cover up. Guarding every word so nobody knew Aunt Junie and I were broke and living in a car and washing our underwear in a truck stop bathroom. I wished I could be even half as courageous as Megan.

"That's getting pretty big."

I blinked. "What?"

Megan stood beside me, her body casting a shadow. "Your snowball. We're not gonna be able to lift it if it gets much bigger."

"Oh." I looked at my snow ball, forced myself to focus. "Yeah, you're right." I slowly straightened. "Guess we should do something about that."

Megan bent over and put her arms around one side, and I grasped it from the other. "Okay, ready," she said, "on the count of three. One . . . two . . . three." And together we grunted and groaned and managed to heft the snowball and carry it over to top Megan's base.

"Lookin' great, girls," Trina called. "But no back injuries, please."

Megan giggled. "Aw, don't worry, Trina. Girl power and all, ya' know."

"Yeah," I added. "We're superwomen."

But I knew there was only one superhero here, and it sure wasn't me.

We went inside for lunch—hot cocoa, grilled cheese and tomato soup—and then Trina laid a piece of notebook paper on the table. "Each Saturday I make a list of chores that didn't get done during the week," she explained. "You're not required to do any of them, but each is worth five dollars if you want to earn a little spending money."

I scraped the last little bit of tomato soup from my bowl as I scanned the list. Iron shirts, vacuum, clean bathrooms, Murphy Oil the cabinets, roll dimes.

"Dimes," Todd squealed. "I'm rolling the dimes."

"I'll do the cabinets," Megan said. "I love the smell of the soap."

"I used to help my mom iron sometimes," I said.

Trina brought out the iron and board and set it up in the corner of the kitchen. "Please be careful and don't burn yourself," she said, draping several blouses over a nearby chair. "And don't worry about doing them perfectly. Just do the best you can."

I was waiting for the iron to heat when my phone vibrated. It was Aunt Junie, and I dashed into the bedroom. "Hi, Aunt Junie."

"Hey, Shannon," she said. "It's great to hear your voice. How are you, bug?"

"I'm fine," I said, as a host of emotions swirled through me. "Are you okay?"

"I just had my court appearance, and I don't have long to talk. But I met Miss Kinney. She told me about Trina. Is she nice?"

"Yeah, she's nice. But what did the judge say?"

"He said I have to serve a week in jail. But it's okay, it's totally my fault."

I groaned. A whole week. Seven long days. If I couldn't talk Trina into letting me bring Boone here, maybe she'd at least take me to visit him each day. I had to see him. "So you'll come get me as soon as the week's up, right?"

She took a hesitant breath. "I wish I could, bug, but first I have to go to rehab and complete a three week alcohol education course."

I gasped. "Three weeks!" I barely made it to the bed before my knees crumpled. "But that's too long, Aunt Junie. That's a whole month. What about Boone?"

"Miss Kinney said the humane society's boarding him. He'll be okay there for a while, right?"

I shook my head, gritted my teeth to keep from saying something really mean. "No, he's not okay! I want him with me. I'm not leaving him there for..."

A gruff voice interrupted in the background. "Time to get off now."

"Yes, sir, I know," Aunt Junie said. "But I'm talking to my niece. She's only twelve, please just give us one more minute."

Panic clawed at my chest. "Aunt Junie, wait. You can't go yet. What am I supposed to do about Boone?"

"Oh, Shannon," her breathing suddenly sounded labored. "I'm sorry. I know it sounds like a long time, but he'll be fine. Now listen, I won't have my phone in jail so I might not be able to talk with you this week, but I promise I'll call you the very next chance I get, okay?"

"But wait... what if something happens? What if I need to...?"

"I have to hang up. I'm sorry, bug. Talk with you soon."

And just like that she was gone.

I sat on the bed, gripping my phone in one hand and the stuffed lamb in the other while my heart threatened to pound right out of my chest. There was a name for that—Tachycardia. I'd never read about a twelve year old having a heart attack, but maybe I would be the first.

For the past two years Aunt Junie and Boone had been my whole family—pretty much my whole world. It was like falling asleep someplace safe and familiar, and waking up in a foreign country. What in the world was I supposed to do now?

But only a few minutes later, my panicky feeling began to fade, shoved aside by a fury I'd never felt before. This whole stinking mess was not right. It was *not* fair. Aunt Junie deserved what she got. But Boone didn't. Boone was counting on me.

And nobody was going to keep me from my dog.

CHAPTER TWELVE

I WASN'T SURE I'D go to school while I was at Trina's, but Miss Kinney called Sunday evening to say she'd pick me up in the morning. I was secretly glad because it would make my plan much easier.

I'd spent most of the day studying Google Maps and figuring out the best way to rescue Boone. The humane society was four miles from Logan Elementary. As soon as school let out tomorrow afternoon I'd catch a city bus that would take me within a quarter mile of Boone. Less than two blocks from there was Spalding's Marine Salvage, a huge field littered with abandoned boats of every shape and size. I'd find a safe spot for us to hide out until one of three things happened—Trina agreed to let me keep Boone at her house, Miss Kinney found us someplace else to stay, or Aunt Junie finished rehab and came to get me. I prayed it would be one of the first two, because nearly four weeks sounded like a really long time to hide out.

Sunday evening, I filled my back pack with carefully selected items—two sweatshirts and a pair of leggings, a tightly rolled fleece blanket, a short piece of clothesline to use for Boone's leash, a roll of toilet paper, a tiny bar of hotel soap and a Sudoku puzzle book from Mitzi. Late that night, once Trina had gone to bed and Megan snored, I crept out to the kitchen. I slapped together a peanut butter and jelly sandwich, then gathered a baggie full of Graham crackers, two oranges, two cheese sticks, a banana and three of Trina's blueberry muffins. It wasn't much, but my backpack was already bulging. Hopefully, it would get us through for a while.

When Miss Kinney picked me up the next morning, I politely answered her questions, but kept my face toward the window the rest of the time. I figured the less said, the less chance she'd sense something was up.

She dropped me off ten minutes before the bell, and I spotted Mitzi sitting on the cement planter where I'd waited for Aunt Junie a few days earlier. Seeing her made me feel like I was being pulled apart. She'd been a friend to me when none of the other kids wanted to be. Now I was going to repay her by vanishing into thin air, just like Amber had done to me. I promised myself I'd make it right with her just as soon as Aunt Junie got a job and we had a real place to live again.

I snuck over and poked her shoulder from behind. "Boo!"

"Hey," she yelped, as the notebook flew from her hands. But then her scowl dissolved into a grin. "Whoa … Shannon. I was just thinking about you, and poof, here you are."

I giggled. "You must be a pretty powerful thinker." I scooped up her notebook and brushed the smear of snow from its polka dot cover.

"Thanks. Hey, are you busy this Saturday? I was hoping maybe we could hang out. You could come over, or I could ask my mom if I could come to your house."

I suddenly felt like I was choking. "Saturday?" I asked brightly. "Um … that'd be great, only I can't. I've gotta do chores."

Her face scrunched. "Chores? Booooring."

"I know. But we've got some company coming, and I promised my aunt I'd help her clean the house."

Mitzi hurled a sigh at me. "Can't you do it before then? My parents have to work Saturday, and I'll be stuck home with nothing to do."

"Oh, yeah?" I said, grasping at the chance to change the subject. "What do they do for work?"

"Mom's a realtor, but she works from home except for two Saturdays when she has to go to the office. Dad drives a forklift." Her brown eyes lit up. "Hey, I know. I could come help you clean. It'd be way more fun that way."

"Yeah, but I don't think my aunt would go for it. Maybe the following Saturday."

Her shoulders slumped. "Bummer," she said. "Where do you live anyway?"

My stomach twisted into a knot. "Where do I live?"

"Um ... yeah," she said, giggling. "Where do you, like, reside?"

I struggled to come up with a street name. *Any* street name. "You know where the Flying J truck stop is? Over near there."

Mitzi did a double take. "That far? How'd you end up at this school?"

I shrugged. "I dunno. This is where my aunt registered me."

"Hmm. That's weird."

I wanted to ask what was so weird about it, but I was afraid it would only lead to more questions. A couple of younger girls played four-square nearby and the ball bounced over and whacked me on the knee. I tossed it back. Mitzi still looked puzzled. "You like dogs?" I asked quickly.

Her eyebrows peaked. "Yeah, they're okay. Why?"

"Because I've got a Jack Russell," I said, digging my phone from my pocket. "He's super cute. Look."

"Awww," she said. "He's gorgeous."

I let her scroll through my pictures while I focused on the four-square players. They had to be the lousiest players ever, the ball hit the line nearly every time.

"Hey," Mitzi said, "is this your house?" She held my phone up.

It was a picture of Boone outside our cabin in Plummer, hunting bumblebees in a clump of daffodils near the front porch. I'd taken it last spring and seeing it now washed me with homesickness. "Yeah," I said, softly. "That's my house."

The bell rang and Mitzi tossed me the phone. "I wanna see the rest of your pics later."

"Okay," I said, and we both joined the torrent of kids funneling into the building. I scooted into Mrs. Stedman's class with my head down and ran smack into Levi. I jumped back, startled. "Whoa, sorry."

He sneered at the bright splashes of color on my tie-dye shirt. "Nice shirt," he said, "looks like you hurled on it."

My face flamed. "Shut up," I snapped, stepping around him. The words came out louder than I planned, and Mrs. Stedman raised her eyebrows. "Good morning, you two. How about trying to be a little nicer to each other."

Levi skittered away with a smirk, and I hated myself for wasting an apology on him. *Jerk!* I slipped into my seat with my nose burning. Another day off to a spectacular start.

"Okay, boys and girls," Mrs. Stedman called. "Take your seats, please. I hope everybody had a good weekend." She handed a stack of papers to Bethany. "You're my class helper today, so can you please hand everyone their history tests back while I take attendance?"

Mine glided across my desk with a slight whoosh, a red C glaring at me from the top of the paper. *Not bad,*

Mrs. Stedman had written. *But was it your best effort?* I lowered my eyes. She was right. I hadn't even studied. She'd probably never believe I used to be a straight-A student. I folded the test and shoved it in my desk.

"Right after I finish attendance, we'll be starting our unit on the Constitution and the Declaration of Independence," she said. "It's really interesting, and I think everyone will enjoy it."

Kiera's hand shot up. "Did you know kids can declare independence from their parents if they want to? I saw it on some show my dad was watching last night."

Mrs. Stedman nodded. "Well, there is something called an emancipated minor."

"Yeah, yeah, that was it," Kiera said. "An emancipated minor."

Levi smirked. "Did you just say you're a constipated minor?"

I wasn't about to laugh at anything Levi said, but everybody else cracked up, and Kiera blushed the color of a ripe strawberry. Mrs. Stedman put her hand over her mouth, which made everybody laugh all the harder. She had to raise both hands to regain control. "Okay, okay," she said. "I think we better avoid potty humor and stick to the topic at hand. Everyone needs to read their library books for a few minutes until I'm ready."

She sat at her desk, and the air filled with the sound of backpacks unzipping and papers rustling. I propped my head on my hand and stared at my desk. I couldn't read my library book. It was in the trunk of the Impala—wherever *that* was. I wondered how long it might be before I got it back. Hopefully before it was overdue.

"Shannon?" Mrs. Stedman gestured to me. "Could you come here a minute?" She waited for me to approach and then pointed to her attendance clipboard. "Do you have a note for your absence last Friday?"

A note? Last Friday seemed like forever ago. "Oh, um … no."

"Well, you weren't sick again all ready, were you?"

My mind turned mushy. "No," I said. "I just … we had some car problems, and by the time we got it fixed it was too late to come."

"I see." Mrs. Stedman pursed her lips and nodded, but she didn't seem very convinced. She leaned toward me. "Is everything okay, Shannon?" she asked, her voice low. "Is there anything you'd like to talk about?"

"No," I said. "I'm fine. I just forgot to remind my aunt to write me a note."

She puffed out a small breath, and I could tell she was disappointed. "All right. I'm just concerned because you're behind on quite a few assignments and it's negatively affecting your grades. If you can't turn things around quickly," she paused, as if she wanted to be sure she had my attention, "I'll have to give you a D in both English and Math for the quarter."

I swallowed, stunned. I knew I was getting behind, but not *that* behind. I'd never had a grade below B on any report card. "D?" I echoed.

She bit her lip and nodded.

"Okay," I said. "I'll work harder on trying to make stuff up."

"Good. And make sure you bring a note tomorrow. In the meantime, you'll need to go and ask Officer Murphy for a temporary pass."

The hair on the back of my neck stood up. "What? How come?"

"Because without one I can't mark your absence as approved, and you're not supposed to be in class with an unapproved absence. Just explain to him about the car problems and I'm sure he'll give you a pass."

"Right," I said, because what else was there to say? I glanced at Mitzi as I turned, but she was focused on her book. Not that it really mattered, she wasn't going to be able to save me again anyway. The crickets performed circus acts in my stomach as I crept down the hall. I should've ditched school and went to get Boone this morning.

Officer Murphy used a small room beside the main office, and I could hear him talking on the phone as I reached his door. He leaned forward in a creaky wooden desk chair, his phone in one hand and a pen in the other. And right on the edge of his desk was the big box of tissues I'd heard about. My hands started to sweat.

I hovered in the doorway, not sure what to do. He hadn't seen me yet and he was busy. What would happen if I went back and told Mrs. Stedman that he was on the phone and couldn't give me a pass? It was worth a shot. I eased back toward the vending machine, a half step at a time. I'd almost made my escape when he glanced up and caught me—a perfect repeat of the day at the Flying J. His eyes widened for a second before he waved me in and pointed to the folding chair in front of his desk.

I shuffled over and perched on the edge of the metal seat, pinning my hands between my knees to keep them from shaking. The potted fern atop his file cabinet looked exactly like the fern we had in our kitchen back home. It was Mom's favorite plant and she babied it something awful, making sure it had enough light, dusting its lacy fronds, giving it a dropper full of Miracle Grow every week. Now the poor thing was stuck in the cold, dark shed with the rest of our stuff. I felt a pang in my chest when I thought how miserable it must be out there—even more miserable than the palm at the police department. I hoped it could survive.

Officer Murphy slipped his phone into the chest pocket of his shirt looking genuinely happy to see me. "Hey, there. How's the Sun Chips girl?"

I know it was probably silly, but there were 600 kids at Logan Elementary, and the fact that he remembered my favorite snack touched me somewhere deep inside. "Good," I said.

"Yeah? And how about your aunt Junie, still job hunting?"

"No," I said, without even thinking. "She got hired at Costco."

One corner of his mouth twitched into a half smile before he straightened it again, like he was surprised in a good way but didn't want me to know for some reason. "Costco, huh? Good for her. So what can I do for you?"

"Mrs. Stedman sent me to get a temporary pass ... for last Friday."

"Ah, no note, huh?"

"Aunt Junie didn't write me one. I forgot to remind her."

"Mmm," he said, like he wasn't quite sure how to react, and I was tempted to explain that all he needed to do was give me the pass and send me on my way. Instead, he folded his hands and regarded me with a curious look. "How come you were absent?"

He had hazel eyes, the same color as Mom's. I'd never noticed it before. I focused on the fern instead. "We had a problem with our car."

"That's too bad. What was wrong with it?"

I smashed my hands even harder between my knees. What did he think I was, a mechanic? "Um ... it wouldn't run."

He chuckled. "Really? That's a problem all right."

"It wouldn't start, is what I meant."

"Hmm. You found a shop to fix it over the weekend, huh?"

"Huh?"

"Well, it's Monday now. So if you had the problem Friday, then you must have gotten it fixed over the weekend."

"Oh, well ... " I shook my head, suddenly flustered. "It was actually fixed on Friday, but it took a while, you know?"

"So you didn't come to school because you didn't get the car back in time."

"Yeah," I said, softly. "It was pretty late."

Officer Murphy picked up his pen and tapped it against his palm with a thoughtful look. "You know what's interesting, Shannon?" He swiveled his screen toward me and with a few clicks of the mouse brought up a graph. "Take a look at your record." He pointed to the furthest column on the right. Curiosity made me inch forward.

"This is your record from the first quarter of the school year before you moved here. You went the whole time without being late or absent even once. But since you've been here ... " He moved his cursor over one column. " ... You've missed eight days, but not in a row, and you've been late six times. Know what that tells me?"

I'd been sweating the whole time, but now my entire body felt like it was melting under the heat of a giant spotlight. Did he expect an answer? Or was it one of those rhetorical questions Mrs. Stedman had taught us about? I shook my head.

"It tells me either something's been going on at school or at home. Which is it?"

"Neither," I said quickly. "It was just the move, and then I caught a bad cold and the thing happened with the car. And ... I don't even remember for sure why I was late those times."

He studied me. "I know Junie drinks, Shannon. Is that what's been interfering with school?"

I pushed back in my chair with a racing heart. Tachycardia again. "No. No, everything's fine, really."

"I can help you if you tell me what's going on."

I took a huge breath. Here I'd thought he was such a nice guy, but what he really wanted was to trap me. But why? He had hundreds of kids to deal with, why did he care what was going on with me and Aunt Junie? And like a sudden flame, a memory sparked to life—the day I'd run into him at the Flying J. He'd remembered Aunt Junie's first name. And they'd acted so weird to each other, like they were having a slugging match with their eyes. I'd bought Aunt Junie's story about being spooked because she'd been sleeping ... until now. Now I realized I'd been a fool. There had to be more to the story.

I swallowed. "Officer Murphy, were you and Aunt Junie ever ..." His penetrating gaze cut me off mid-sentence, paralyzing me for a few seconds. But I had to know. I pushed forward. "What I was wondering is, did you guys know each other before the day I registered for school?"

He set his jaw and looked away before I even finished the question, and I instantly recognized what he was doing. He was gritting his teeth to keep from saying what he really wanted to. It was so familiar, because I did it all the time. And it filled me with the strangest floaty sensation.

He tapped the pen against his palm a few more times, then abruptly opened a drawer and pulled out a yellow form. He scrawled the date on top and his name on the bottom and slid it across to me. "Here's your pass," he said. "Go ahead back to class."

I blinked at the pass and then up at him. He hadn't answered my question, but I hadn't answered his either. It was a tie. I took the pass and stood. "Thank you," I said, with as much dignity as I could muster. And I walked out of his office with my chin raised.

CHAPTER THIRTEEN

I PASTED ON A bored expression as I walked into class and laid my pass on Mrs. Stedman's desk. Mitzi caught my eye and jiggled her brows, probably wondering what had taken so long. I flashed her a confident smile as I slid into my chair, but it didn't quiet the tremor in my hands.

Mrs. Stedman chattered about the Second Amendment, how important it was to us as a nation. But right then I couldn't remember what the Second Amendment even was. I was too busy puzzling over Officer Murphy. He was a mystery. And mysteries scared me silly.

The day dragged on forever, but the dismissal bell finally rang, and I fled out the door with a single focus—get Boone. I jogged across the street and slipped behind the tall row of evergreen shrubs lining the sidewalk, hiding myself from the long line of cars in the pick-up lane where

Miss Kinney surely waited. Then I cut catty corner across the next street until I was out of sight of the school.

I trotted two blocks to the transit stop marked on my phone and then paced back and forth behind the covered bus stop bench, as tense as a cat listening to a mouse in the wall. How hard would it be to get Boone out of the shelter? What would Miss Kinney do when I didn't show up? I hoped Trina wouldn't get in trouble. What would Officer Murphy think when I was absent again tomorrow? When would Aunt Junie find out I was missing? What would she think? And what about poor Mitzi?

A grey city bus huffed to a stop a few minutes later and as soon as I clambered up the steps I felt bigger and stronger, like I'd experienced an instant growth spurt. I found an empty seat and crushed up against the window clutching my backpack. I tingled all over with the prospect of finally getting to hold Boone again, to pet him and kiss him. To tell him how sorry I was for letting him be taken away.

It was three-thirty by the time the bus dropped me off near the river, and I hiked along the marina's wooden boardwalk, past all the empty boat slips and the skeleton Ferris wheel. The humane society was a cedar sided building with white trim and a huge paw print painted on the front entrance. I eagerly pushed through the glass doors.

An old lady with short brown hair limped across the lobby carrying a plate of cookies. "Well, goodness," she said, startled. "Someone's in a hurry." She set the cookies next to a gurgling pot of coffee. "What can I do for you, dear?"

"I'm Shannon," I said. "I'm here to pick up my dog, Boone."

"I see." She furrowed her brow. "Is there someone here with you?"

"Oh, sure," I said, jabbing a thumb over my shoulder. "My aunt's waiting in the car. She had a phone call to make."

"Oh, of course," she said, shuffling behind the counter. "I'm only a volunteer, so I should probably check with someone before I ... "

"Helen knows," I blurted. "She said I could pick him up anytime."

Her face relaxed. "Oh, you've already spoken with Helen? Oh, lovely then. What is your last name, dear?"

"O'Reilly."

The lady shook her finger. "Ahh, a good Irish name. Hold on now, I'm not too speedy when it comes to typing." She bent over a computer and pecked at the keyboard with one finger. It was all I could do to keep from vaulting over the reception counter and doing it for her.

"Oh ... yes," she said eventually. "Sure enough. Shannon O'Reilly. Hold on just a minute."

"Okay. Thanks." I drummed my fingers on the counter and prayed she'd gone to get Boone and not to make some secret phone call to report me. I studied the happy looking terrier on the banner above my head. *I'll be your Forever Friend! Adopt me today.* I edged over to the plate of chocolate chip cookies, wrapped two in a napkin and stuck them in the pocket of my sweatshirt. After what seemed like a year, the lady hobbled back with Boone tucked under her arm. He hadn't spotted me yet, and he held his ears flat, like he wasn't sure what to expect.

My chest swelled. "Boone," I called, "Hey, Boone."

His ears jumped to attention and his little head whipped toward me. His whole body rocked as he tried to claw his way free of the lady's grip. "Oh, goodness," she said. "Hang on now."

I rushed over and grabbed him in my arms. He licked my hands like a madman, whimpering with urgency, as if he had a year's worth of stories to tell me all at once.

I couldn't remember ever feeling so relieved. "I know," I murmured. "I know, boy. I missed you too."

"Oh, my," the lady said, clicking her tongue. "That's one happy little dog."

I kissed him on top of the head and raised my face out of the way of his tongue. "Thank you so much," I said. "Tell Helen I said thank you too."

"You bet." She wiggled her fingers at Boone. "So long little fella."

"I better go," I said, "my aunt's waiting." I hoisted my backpack over a shoulder and rushed out, terrified the lady would think of some excuse to stop me. But she didn't say anything more than "goodbye," and I escaped through the glass door to freedom.

I scurried around behind the building and knelt to dig out the clothesline from Trina's. I forced one end through the loop on Boone's collar and tied a knot, which was pretty much like tying your shoe while doing jumping jacks with the way Boone was leaping around. "Stop," I scolded. "We have to get out of here first. Then you can tell me the whole story, okay?"

Spalding's Marine Salvage was housed in a huge steel warehouse, a field of boats spread out behind, the whole property secured by a tall wooden fence plastered with No Trespassing signs. Fortunately, it was an old fence with lots of missing slats, and it wasn't hard to find a gap to squirm through. I paused inside, holding tight to Boone's clothes-line, and listening to the rumble and revving of heavy equipment. I surveyed the graveyard of boats. Most were old and rusty, with cracked hulls, missing engines and broken cabin windows. But some looked in surprisingly good shape, like they should be snug in winter storage instead of out here. "Where should we go, boy?" I whispered, even though I didn't see anyone around to overhear.

Boone looked up at me, his eyes dancing with excitement, like it was the best adventure of his life. "Come on," I said, tromping through the dirty snow to a blue and white houseboat sticking out among a group of smaller boats. A boat like that would offer plenty of room to move around, and it even had curtains to keep anyone from spying. I lifted Boone up on the deck and then hoisted myself through the metal railing before cautiously stepping inside the cabin.

The white panel ceiling bulged in places and the floor was littered with grime and yellow tufts of insulation. It smelled of dampness, and the cabin door was jammed open so there was no way to block the cold air. But it had a sturdy table with a bench seat, and a bed with a thick pad. The cabinets still housed a few old pans and a clock hung on the wall, its hands stopped at 1:47. There was even a bathroom with a toilet and mini sink. I grinned at Boone. "What do you think, boy? Not too shabby, huh?"

I gave the mattress a test bounce and Boone sailed onto my lap. I ran my fingers through his warm fur, so happy to be able to hold him even though he stunk like the shelter. "We're definitely not homeless now," I said. "We have our very own houseboat. Only rich people have houseboats. Did you know that, Boone? Pretty cool, huh?"

He washed my chin in agreement and I giggled. "Guess what else we've got?" I pulled the napkin from my pocket. "Cookies to celebrate. But let's get settled first, okay?"

I emptied out my backpack and set our food on the table out of Boone's reach. "Come on," I said, "let's explore our boat." Boone followed at my heels as I peered onto shelves and into cabinets. I found a braided nylon rope, three life vests, some pens and paper, an old metal can opener and a baggie full of screws and nails. Nothing too exciting, but there were lots of other boats to explore.

My first job was to figure out how to close the cabin door so I could let Boone off his leash. I squatted down for a closer look. A piece of metal trim had peeled back from the bottom of the door and stuck into the wooden deck like a door stop. Kicking it free didn't work, neither did trying to stomp it flat. Finally I grabbed it with both hands and forced it to bend up. It snapped in half and I fell backwards. Boone's look of alarm made me laugh. "It's okay," I said. "I'm fine."

I climbed back to my feet and gave the door a shove. It swung closed and I clapped my hands. "Check it out, boy. I fixed it. No sweat." I had just untied the clothesline from his collar when my phone sounded. *Rebecca Kinney.* Boone's ears peaked like he knew I should answer it, but I shook my head. "We can't. We're fugitives, remember?"

Miss Kinney called three more times over the next two hours while I watched a crane lift a yacht off a semi-truck. Two guys in hard hats trotted around waving their arms and trying to direct the crane operator. A few other workers stood around talking on phones, their voices drowned out by the clanking and beeping of equipment moving in and out of the giant warehouse. I'd just headed over to get the peanut butter and jelly sandwich when my phone rang again.

Aunt Junie

I stood paralyzed with indecision. How could Aunt Junie be calling? She was in jail. She wouldn't have her phone, would she? I grabbed it right before it went to voice mail. "Hello?"

"Shannon! Are you okay?"

"Hi," I said, wondering how much she knew. "I'm good. How are you?"

"I got a call from Miss Kinney saying you weren't there after school and you didn't show up at Trina's. No one knows where you are."

I couldn't help smiling. "I'm sorry," I lied. "I was gonna text you. I didn't think you'd find out so fast."

"Find out what? Where are you?"

"I … I'm with Boone, Aunt Junie."

There was a long pause. "With Boone? You ran away to visit him at the humane society?"

"I had to," I said. "I had to get him out of there."

"Out of there?" she echoed, her voice rising. "You took him and went somewhere? Where are you, Shannon?"

I clenched the phone. "I can't tell you. Nobody can know. They'll take Boone back to the shelter. I can't keep him at Trina's because one of the kids has bad allergies. I didn't know what else to do."

"Oh … Jeez, bug." Aunt Junie's voice clogged with frustration. "You have to tell me where you are."

"I can't," I said. "Not until I figure out a way for me and Boone to stay together."

"I won't tell. Not as long as I know you're somewhere safe. You have to trust me, Shannon."

I swallowed. "I do trust you. But this time you have to trust me, okay? You can call me and … "

"I can't," she interrupted. "They only let me use my phone this time because Miss Kinney convinced the officers you might pick up if you saw the call was from me. I can't do anything for another four days."

Panic shot through me at the word *officers*. What if they traced my phone? "I'm fine, Aunt Junie. I promise. We're together, and we've got food and we're safe. Call me as soon as you get out. Love you. Bye."

I rushed through the last three words and hung up before she had a chance to say anything more. The phone instantly rang again, but I didn't answer. I bit my lip and stared at Boone until the phone finally went silent.

CHAPTER FOURTEEN

I SHARED MY SANDWICH with Boone and then worked a couple Sudoku puzzles. I had a third one partly solved when the racket outside abruptly stopped. I flipped over to peek out the window. A fork lift still puttered in the far corner, but the crane was gone, and the rest of the equipment was parked in front of the building. A worker rolled down the big metal door before he hopped in a pickup and drove out the main gate.

The sun was a sinking golden ball in the west and my fingers already quivered with cold. I got scared thinking how low the temperature might drop overnight. Boone and I made eye contact and his stub tail wagged. "Come on," I said. "We have to figure out how to make up our bed so we don't freeze to death tonight."

I pulled on an extra sweatshirt beneath my jacket and lined up the open life vests across the mattress. Then I unrolled the blanket from Trina's, tucking half of it around the vests and leaving the other half free to pull over Boone and me. It looked like a giant, bulky burrito but if we didn't move around too much it would hopefully stay in place and keep us warm enough.

The sun dipped completely out of sight a few minutes later and darkness closed in like an evil black curtain. That's when I realized my first big mistake. No flashlight. I could've kicked myself for overlooking something so important. The only light was the glow from my cell phone, and I didn't dare use it more than I had to. A full charge usually lasted three days, but how long would it last in the cold? Once it went dead how would I charge it again?

I'd never gone to bed at six o'clock in my life, but there wasn't much else to do. I scooped Boone up and set him on the mattress. "Come on," I said, "let's see if we can make this work."

Wriggling onto the life vests without knocking them off was a lot like balancing Jell-O in your hands, but we finally managed it, and I tugged the blanket over us. I gently stroked Boone, feeling exhausted and anxious, but proud too. After all, I'd accomplished a lot today. I'd escaped from school, freed Boone and found us a temporary place to live—all without the help of a single grown up.

It was pitch black when I woke with a start. I lay there shaking and disoriented. The life vests had fallen off and I was freezing. Boone curled tightly against my stomach, his little body radiating the only heat there was. The last thing I wanted was to scoot away from him, but I had to pee really bad. I dug out my phone. *One forty-five.* I wanted to cry when I thought of all the hours until daylight.

I shined the phone at my feet and stumbled to the toilet in the back of the boat. I hadn't planned on using it, but I sure wasn't going outside to find another spot right then. The toilet seat was a block of ice and I gasped when I sat down. At least I'd remembered to pack stupid toilet paper.

I didn't realize Boone had followed me until I stood up and tripped over him. I banged my knee and hollered, and he scrambled away with a yelp. "Sorry, boy. Sorry. Are you okay? C'mere, Boone." I groped around me until I felt his wet tongue on my hand and then scooped him up and kissed his head. "I didn't see you. Are you okay?" I limped back to the bed before sweeping aside the curtain to peek outside.

The view took my breath away.

A bazillion stars glistened like diamonds on black velvet, hovering almost close enough to touch. I'd never seen a night sky so beautiful, not even the time Mom and I slept outside to watch the August meteor showers. I wondered if the night sky always looked this amazing at two o'clock in the morning. If I hadn't been chilled to the bone I would've stared longer, but my whole body shook and my stomach growled besides.

I only planned to eat a couple of the Graham crackers, but they tasted so good I wolfed down nearly the whole baggie full. Then I did my best to rearrange the life vests and blanket and tried to cocoon them back over us. I lay there trembling and miserable, swearing I'd never be warm again, but at some point I stopped shivering and my eyes grew heavy, and I slept.

The rumble of machinery woke me the next time. Light poured through the curtain, and for a few seconds I thought I was at the Flying J with a semi idling next to us. But then I felt Boone smashed against me, and I remembered. I blinked at my phone, surprised to see it was nearly nine thirty. Boone tunneled out of the blanket, bouncing around and trying to lick my face. "Stop," I grumbled. "You're letting cold air in."

But he didn't stop. He hopped to the floor and started doing his potty dance. "Okay, okay," I said, "hold on a sec." I forced myself to sit up and glanced out the window with a yawn. Puffy grey clouds had replaced the beautiful clear night, and I wondered if the stars had really been there or if I'd dreamed the whole thing. The big warehouse door was rolled up again and a forklift revved around a truck towing a damaged aluminum boat. None of the workers were close enough to see us as long as we stayed behind the houseboat.

I fastened the piece of clothesline to Boone's collar before opening the cabin door a few inches to make sure the coast was clear. Then I jumped to the ground and lifted Boone down. He took his time sniffing for a suitable spot to do his business, and I studied the field of boats as I trailed behind him. I wished I had special x-ray vision to see inside them from a distance. No way could I survive another night as awful as the last one. We definitely needed more clothes or covers, and some kind of light so we didn't have to endure fourteen hours of darkness.

Once Boone finished I hurried him back to the houseboat for breakfast. We shared one of Trina's blueberry muffins and a cheese stick. He wagged his tail hopefully as I brushed muffin crumbs from my sweatshirt. "I know," I said, "I want another one too, but we have to make our food last. Let's go exploring and see what we can find."

I carefully peeked out the door again and jerked back. A worker was welding nearby, his torch sending up a spray of sparks like fireworks, and I was afraid we'd never make it past him without being seen. I paced impatiently, checking every few minutes until he finally headed back to the warehouse, lugging a suitcase sized chunk of metal on his shoulder. "Okay," I told Boone. "I think it's safe now. Let's go. But be quiet, okay?"

He danced around like he understood and we slipped through the cabin door and hopped to the ground. "Let's check out that big sailboat over there," I said, pointing.

The tall mast of the sailboat was broken in half, and the cabin tilted, but it barely looked damaged. I pushed Boone through an open window and then squeezed after him. The rear of the cabin was black and charred as if the engine had caught fire, but the front hadn't been touched. I discovered a book of poetry in one of the cabinets, its pages stiff and crinkly from moisture, and two dollars and fifty six cents in a little coffee jar under the sink. But the best find was a fleece Seattle Seahawks blanket folded in the captain's chair. The top part was discolored by the sun but there was nothing else wrong with it.

I squirmed back through the window with my treasures and waited for Boone to hop out. "Come on," I said, "let's check out another one." I didn't find anything worth keeping on the next several boats, but there was a working cigarette lighter and a weather radio on the big aluminum fishing boat on the end. The radio didn't have batteries, but I decided to take it in case I found some later.

It was lunchtime when we snuck back to our houseboat, and I was trying to figure out how best to dole out our food when my phone rang. *Mitzi.* Instinct told me not to answer, but I really wanted to. "Hey, Mitzi."

"Hey," she said. "Are you okay? You're not here again."

I sighed. "I know. I just … something came up."

"Something came up," she repeated, incredulous. "I thought you wanted to go to school to be a doctor. It's not gonna look very good if you fail sixth grade."

Her words gave me a jolt. "I'm not going to fail sixth grade."

"So what came up?"

I didn't answer. What was I supposed to say?

"Shannon?"

"I can't tell you," I said.

"Why not?" she asked, sounding hurt. "I can keep my mouth shut."

"I wish I could. I just … can't right now."

"Well, are you okay? Did something weird happen?"

"I'm okay. But listen, I might not be at school for a little while. I'll be back as soon as I can, though."

"Where are you?"

I puffed out another breath. "That's what I can't tell you. Nobody knows where I am right now."

"Nobody knows …" Mitzi gasped. "Wait. You ran away?"

"Yep."

"OMG! Why? Were you like, being abused or something?"

"No, nothing like that. It's just a really long story."

"Well, guess what? I've got eight whole minutes until the bell rings, so ready, set, GO!"

I laughed. I couldn't help it. Mitzi always made me laugh when I least expected it. It was my favorite thing about her. It's also what made me so sad we couldn't be the kind of friends I wanted us to be. "I don't think you'd believe me if I told you," I said.

"Try me."

Boone reached out a front leg and patted my knee and I squeezed his paw. "I can't, Mitzi. Not yet. Maybe in a while..."

"I could help you."

"How?"

"I dunno. Don't you need stuff if you're alone?"

Yes, I wanted to say. *I need a flashlight, and more blankets and food, and a heater would be nice too.* "I'm not alone," I said. "I have Boone." There was a pause after that. The forklift was still running around, closer than before, and I pulled back the curtain.

"Soooo," Mitzi said, "you're hiding out someplace with your dog and you don't need anything?"

"Not yet. It's just the second day."

"Can you at least tell me if you're still here in Logan?"

"Yep, I'm still here."

"All right," she huffed. "Well, I'm calling you as soon as I get home from school tomorrow whether you want me to or not. Just to see if you're okay and stuff."

My heart swelled a little. "Actually, I'd like that," I said. "As long as my phone doesn't die."

"Okay. And you promise to tell me what's going on as soon as you can?"

I nodded, even though she couldn't see me. "Thanks for being my friend, Mitzi. Talk to you tomorrow."

I scooped Boone up and gave him a hug. "Good thing I have you," I said. "Ready for lunch?" I set him on the mattress and crawled on beside him, and we shared another of Trina's blueberry muffins and an orange. I wished I'd smuggled out more muffins. I tried not to think about the pile of French toast and bacon and eggs she'd made for breakfast the other day.

CHAPTER FIFTEEN

I SPENT A LAZY afternoon paging through the book of
poetry and trying not to worry about running out of
food. I was thirsty too, I hadn't been smart enough
to bring any water. At least the animal shelter was only a
few blocks away, tomorrow I'd sneak back there and hope
they had more cookies and maybe something to drink.

I worked Sudoku puzzles until the setting sun filled the
cabin with dark eerie shapes and the workers went home
again. Boone and I shared the banana and the last cookie
for dinner before I took him outside for a bathroom break.
Then I folded the Seattle Seahawks blanket in half and we
snuggled down under the comforting weight of the dou-
bled fleece. I dozed off right as the sky begin to spit rain.

The phone startled me awake the next morning. I'd
slept a little better than the first night, but my eyes still felt

like they were filled with gravel as I blinked at my phone. It was 8:40 and it was Aunt Junie calling.

"Hello," I croaked.

"Shannon ... bug, are you okay?"

I cleared my throat. "I'm fine, I just woke up. I didn't think you could call again."

"They're only letting me because of Miss Kinney," she said. "She's here with me, and I want you to tell me where you are so she can come get you."

I sat up and rubbed my eyes as Boone clawed his way out from under the blanket. "No," I said. "I'm not telling anybody."

"Cut it out, Shannon. This is not a joke."

Anger sparked through me and I came fully awake. "I don't think it's a joke, either. But I'm never giving Boone up again."

"Nobody asked you to give him up," she said. "It's only temporary, until I can finish rehab. Then I'll find a job, maybe I can start working at Costco, and I'll find us ... "

"You should already be working at Costco," I interrupted. "Remember, Aunt Junie? That's where we were headed when we got in the accident." My frustration spewed out with a force that surprised me. "And if you hadn't been drinking, there never would've been any accident. And you wouldn't be in jail. And I wouldn't be out here ... by myself." Tears snuck up and made my throat burn.

Aunt Junie took a shuddering breath. "I get all that, Shannon. Believe me, I get it. But you're too young to be alone. It's not safe. You need to tell Miss Kinney..."

"Ask her if I can keep Boone."

"She's just trying to do her job, bug. She can't..."

"Ask her," I demanded.

Aunt Junie sighed. Her voice grew quiet as she turned from the phone, but I could still hear every word. "She wants to know if she can keep her dog if she tells us where she is."

"I'm not going to promise something I can't deliver," Miss Kinney said. "It would only make things worse."

Aunt Junie cleared her throat. "Bug, she says..."

"It's okay," I said. "I heard her. At least she's being honest."

"Shannon," Aunt Junie's voice took on a steely edge. "Now you listen to me. I understand why you're upset. You've got the right. But you're a child, okay. You don't get to make the decisions. Now tell me where you are. Right now."

I pinched my nose, fighting to keep my anger from swallowing me whole. "You don't get to make the decisions right now either, Aunt Junie. You're in jail." I hung up, and jammed the phone back in my pocket.

Boone danced in front of the cabin door, twirling on his hind feet like a ballerina. I shoved my feet into my shoes and took him outside as the pattering raindrops became a shower.

Rain pounded all morning. Once in a while it turned to hail, little pellets of ice bouncing like super balls before warming back to rain. The big warehouse door was open, but I didn't see any of the workers outside, and who could blame them? There was no way to attempt a run to the animal shelter in this mess. Boone and I shared the last blueberry muffin for breakfast, and the last orange and cheese stick for lunch.

I forced myself to work another Sudoku puzzle, but I couldn't quit thinking about Aunt Junie. I'd never said mean things to her like that before. And even though my words were true, and saying them felt good at the time, I didn't feel so good now. I felt like I had an army of tiny feet kicking around inside my head.

The rain finally eased around three o'clock, but the clouds still hung gray and menacing, like they couldn't wait to dump more rain any moment. I took a chance, heading out for a little more exploring. But after only a few minutes I knew it was another bad decision to add to my growing list. The ground was a squishy, disgusting swamp, covered with mud puddles that hid their brown goo below a paper thin layer of ice. Rain puddled in every nook and cranny of every boat.

By the time Boone and I got back to the houseboat, I was soaked and miserable and colder than ever. Even Boone shivered, his thick hair stiff and clumped, his legs coated in mud. I hadn't even found anything worth my effort except for two folded up plastic garbage bags and a couple of cotton dishtowels. I used one of the towels to wipe Boone off the best I could before he hopped back up on the bed.

I peeled off my wet jeans and slipped on my leggings before wrapping myself in the Seattle Seahawks blanket, but I still couldn't quit shaking. I also couldn't stop thinking about the cookies and hot coffee at the humane society. From as far back as I could remember Mom had shared her morning coffee with me—Folgers, sweetened with yummy hazelnut creamer. And right then, I would've given practically everything I owned for a hot mug of it.

Then I realized it was four o'clock and my spirits sank even lower. School had been out for an hour, and Mitzi hadn't called. I'd thought sure she would, that she really did care about me. But apparently she had better things to do, and disappointment settled in my stomach like a rock. I pictured all the kids in my class, dressed in their perfect clothes, on their way back to their perfect homes. They'd go to basketball practice, or dance class, or hang out with friends. Or maybe they'd just stretch out on their perfect beds and hang out online. And I didn't understand what I'd ever done so wrong that I couldn't be just like them.

I stared at my phone, willing it to ring. I wanted to talk to somebody. Anybody. I could call Trina. She'd been so nice to me. If it wasn't for Boone, I'd be at her house now. I'd be warm and dry and not hungry. Maybe if I promised to keep him in the bedroom, away from Todd, she'd let me keep him. Maybe if I begged.

Boone studied me through his big black eye patch, a sliver of tongue sticking out, and I closed my eyes. For the first time, the reality of what I'd done wrapped around me like a suffocating fog, and I didn't feel proud or brave or excited at all anymore. Boone and I were alone in the freezing cold, in a boat salvage yard, with another night of endless darkness just an hour away.

All we had left for food were three Graham crackers. It would get us through tonight, but what about tomorrow? Or the next day? Even if I could get more cookies from the animal shelter, it wouldn't be enough. Aunt Junie still had three weeks of rehab ahead of her. Three weeks— twenty-one days. Her chances of winning a Silver Heart scholarship were almost zero now, which meant she'd have to find some other job. And even if she managed to get hired at Costco, how long would it take to save up two thousand dollars for a place of our own? It could be weeks or even months. It could be never.

I covered my face with my hands and started to cry. Boone leaped onto my lap and forced his nose under my hands to lick my chin. I rubbed my cheek against his head and closed my eyes. "I wish you could talk," I whispered. "I wish you could tell me what to do, Boone. I don't know what to do." We crawled onto the bed, and I pulled the blanket over my head and curled my body tight around Boone.

It was pitch dark when Boone's growl startled me awake.

He balanced on the edge of the mattress, hackles raised, sniffing the air in between growls. My heart jumped into my throat. "What's wrong, boy? What is it?"

I fumbled for my phone. Six-ten. I'd napped for two hours. I forced myself to sit up and that's when I caught a whiff of cigarette smoke. My whole body filled with pins and needles.

I put a trembling hand on Boone. "It's okay," I whispered. "It's okay, boy." But I'm not sure why I said it, because every instinct told me things were not okay at all. I lifted the edge of the curtain but there were no stars tonight, no light at all. I raised my cell phone. My battery was down to 5 percent and barely gave off a glow. Nothing looked any different, but the cigarette smoke was coming from somewhere close ... from *someone* close.

A terrifying thought slammed into me. Those things I'd found on other boats—the lighter and towels, the money and blanket—maybe they hadn't been accidently left behind at all. Maybe they belonged to other people. People who were hiding out just like us. There could be strangers all around me—criminals even, like the man who'd grabbed my arm at the homeless shelter—just waiting for the cover of darkness to come out.

My breath came in short, sharp gasps. "You can have it back," I said out loud. "You can have it all back."

A horrible screech filled the air, like a giant ripping apart metal, and I almost blacked out from fear. Boone barked so hard he was jumping in place. Heavy footsteps thumped across the deck. I shrank inside myself.

A black shadow stepped into the cabin as a beam of light blinded me. "Anybody here?"

"Get out," I screamed. "Stay away!"

"Shannon?"

I was so sure the stranger was a serial killer it took my terrified brain several seconds to realize he'd said my name. The beam of light swept to the side, and I made out a man dressed in jeans and a black coat. "Shannon, it's okay."

He stepped near enough for me to recognize the familiar shape of his face beneath the baseball cap, and I choked out a sob of relief. "O-officer Murphy?"

"Yeah, kiddo, it's me. And boy am I glad to see you."

My heart still stuttered with fear and left me breathless. "Y-you're not in your uniform."

"Nope." He held out a fist to Boone. "Hey there, little guy. Remember me? You don't need to bark. It's okay." Boone instantly relaxed and started to wag his stub tail.

Officer Murphy swept his flashlight around the cabin. "My Gosh, girl. You're one brave kid."

"What are doing here?" I asked. "How did you find me?"

"Come on," he said, "let's get you two out of here. Then we'll talk."

I was too confused to think. But then my mind cleared enough for a new panic to grip me, and I hugged my arms to my chest. "No. No, I can't. I have to stay with Boone."

"We'll sort things out," he said, firmly, "but not here." He reached for my arm and pulled me to my feet before I had any more chance to protest. "Jeez," he said, "you're like an iceberg." He rubbed my arms hard. "You must really love your dog. Now c'mon."

He lifted Boone and placed him in my arms. Then he grabbed my backpack and shined the light toward the cabin door. He helped me off the boat, and led the way out of the salvage yard. I trudged after him, trying to avoid the worst of the mud and the muck, shaking with fear for Boone.

CHAPTER SIXTEEN

O FFICER MURPHY DROVE a red Jeep instead of his patrol car, and he angled the heat vent toward me after starting the engine. The blast of warmth felt wonderful even though it made me shiver harder at first. I held my frozen fingers up to the vent as he called Miss Kinney and told her I was with him and to let Aunt Junie know. Then he tucked his phone away and raised an eyebrow at me. "How about some dinner?"

"Sure," I said. But when he turned the Jeep toward the shelter, I wrapped an arm around Boone and fumbled for the door handle, ready to bail and run the second he pulled into the parking lot. But we cruised right past the cedar sided building and kept going, and a few blocks later he swung into Happy Jack's Bar and Grill.

"Your pup gonna be okay for a while?" he asked, giving Boone's head a rub. "He won't tear apart my seats or anything?"

"Oh ... no," I said. "He should be fine."

Happy Jack's was buzzing with customers and 50s music, and everything smelled so good it made my knees weak. A hostess showed us to a booth and placed ice water before us, and I immediately gulped down most of my glass. Then I settled against the puffy vinyl bench and tried to decide if I was hallucinating or if I was really, truly sitting here, at a restaurant, having dinner with Officer Murphy.

A waitress swept past carrying a pink milkshake piled high with whipped cream, and it about made me drool because it was exactly what I'd told Aunt Junie I wanted the day we'd dreamed up our favorite dinner. Officer Murphy smiled. "Order one."

"Can I?"

"You can."

Condensation from my water glass dripped onto my lap and my face flamed when I looked down at myself. My sweatshirt was wrinkled and raggedy and covered with dog hair. My leggings were spattered with mud, and one side had a two inch rip that I didn't even remember getting. I could only guess how terrible my hair looked—I hadn't brushed it in three days—and I probably smelled like wet dog on top of it. It made me want to crawl under the table. "I look awful," I said.

Officer Murphy tipped his head. "Don't worry about that. Just decide what you want to eat."

I pretended to study my menu, but I already knew exactly what I wanted—a bacon cheeseburger with a boatload of fries and one of those wonderful milkshakes. Officer Murphy ordered a side of fried mushrooms to get us started, and by the time the waitress brought them I'd stopped shivering and calmed down enough to think half way straight. I was pretty sure I'd never take being warm for granted again.

"What made you come looking for me?" I asked.

He speared a mushroom with his fork. "Child Services filed a missing person report. But Junie had already called me. She was beside herself."

I paused to let the impact of those last four words soak in. "How did you know where to find me?"

His eyes crinkled at the corners. "Wasn't too tough once I knew you'd gone after your dog. Mitzi helped too."

I gave a start. "You talked to Mitzi?"

"Sure. She's the only one I ever see you with at school."

"But I didn't tell her anything."

"Nope. But she told me she heard a fork lift in the background when you girls talked."

I tried to remember. Of course... the forklift. She'd said her dad drove a forklift. No wonder she'd recognized the sound. Instead of being upset, I struggled not to smile, because it explained why she hadn't called. She probably thought I was furious with her for ratting me out. "She's not in trouble, is she? She didn't do anything."

He shook his head and nudged the plate of mushrooms toward me. "Here, help me out."

I'd never been a big mushroom fan, but these were delicious. I nibbled the spicy coating as Officer Murphy took off his ball cap and ran a hand through his hair. He studied the older couple in the next booth before folding his hands and focusing back on me. "If there's one thing I've learned working with kids, it's how smart you guys really are, that you deserve the same respect I expect from you. So I've got something I need to tell you, okay? It's probably gonna freak you out a little."

The mushroom suddenly lost its flavor. I'd been pretty much freaked out since we left Plummer. I wasn't sure I could handle much more. "Is it... bad?" I asked.

One corner of his mouth lifted in a half smile. "Parts of it, yeah. But overall, I think it's pretty great."

I wasn't sure if that made me feel better or not.

He took another glance around before reaching inside his jacket and withdrawing a brown leather wallet. He fished through it for a moment, pulled out a small photograph and slid it across to me.

The picture was creased and dog eared with age, and I lifted it for a closer look. A smug teenage boy in swim trunks, his hands on his hips, stood in between two younger girls who I recognized instantly. "Hey," I said, "that's Mom and Aunt Junie. Where did you get this?"

He tapped the teenage boy. "Know who that is?"

I nodded. "I never met him, but I think it's their big brother, Donny. Mom said he got killed in a motorcycle accident."

Officer Murphy winced. "Is that what she told you?"

I felt the strange sensation of needing to duck, like there was an ax hanging over my head about to fall. "Um…yeah."

"It's not the truth," he said. "He didn't die. He's…me."

I dropped the picture.

He folded his hands and tapped his thumbs together. "I'm your uncle, Shannon. Your uncle Donovan. I went by Donny as a kid."

I laughed. I couldn't help it. "No you're not. You can't be."

He stayed silent, his expression hard to read.

The hair on the back of my neck sprang up. "You can't be," I insisted. "Mom wouldn't lie to me."

"Mothers do whatever it takes to protect their kids."

I searched his face. "What are you talking about? Protect them from what?"

He wiped a hand over his chin. "That's a loaded question," he said. "And to explain, I'm gonna have to admit to some things I'm not proud of. But I'll do my best." He wrapped a hand around his water glass and gave it a shake so the ice clinked. "I was eight when your mom was born, ten when Junie came along. We were never close. Maybe it was the age difference, or maybe I was just too selfish to care about being a big brother. But when I hit my teens I fell in with the wrong crowd, started getting in trouble.

"Long story short, my best friend was a computer whiz, a hacker before most people had even heard the word. He taught me what he knew, made me his partner in crime. And when I was eighteen we got arrested for internet fraud. He tried to pin the whole deal on me, but fortunately the cops were too smart. He got six years in prison for being the mastermind, and I served four years for being his accomplice."

I stared at him, fascinated. "What's fraud?"

"It's when you trick people out of their money. We created a fake charity for people who thought they were donating to the American Kidney Foundation. But the money went straight to an account we'd set up."

"No way. That's ... terrible."

He sniffed. "Yeah, that's an understatement. So by the time I got out of prison, your mom was fourteen and Junie was twelve. Mom and Dad had divorced by then, and they were so ashamed of me I was pretty much disowned. I wasn't allowed any contact with my sisters, even though I wanted it by then. So I moved to Montana and hired on with a logging crew for a few years, trying to save money and get my head straight. That's where I decided I wanted to work with kids, find some way to help 'em get through that same age I was when I got in trouble. So I took some college courses and eventually put myself through the police academy. I was a patrolmen in Billings for seven years, working with at risk kids. But then I found out Faye was sick and I wanted to be closer."

My brain lagged way behind my ears, so it took me a minute to realize he was talking about Mom. I scrunched the napkin in my lap. "How did you find out she was sick?"

"Through a friend," he said. "I always managed to keep some track of what was going on at home. Anyway, not long after, I learned Logan was looking to hire a school resource officer."

"Did you know about me?"

His eyes softened. "I did."

"Then how come you never came to see me in Plummer?"

His mouth turned down. "You'll never know how much I wanted to, Shannon. But I figured if I had any chance of being accepted back into the family, I'd have to prove I really changed. So I made a pact with myself not to contact your mom until I'd done all I could to fix things. But if I'd known just how sick she was, believe me, I would've come."

I'd stopped listening a few sentences back, right after— *you'll never know how much I wanted to. You'll never know how much I wanted to.* I could play that phrase over in my mind a million times and never get tired of it. I struggled to catch up with what he'd said after that. Something about fixing stuff? "Are you talking about the internet fraud thing?"

He nodded. "Once I got out of prison I started tracking down people who'd sent money to the charity we set up. I couldn't find all of them, but I identified a dozen. So little by little over the past ten years I've been paying them back. Another six months or so, and I figured I'd finally be the kind of guy I wanted my niece to know."

I couldn't believe it. He wanted me to know him, he wanted me to like him. I fought to keep my face straight. "How much did you have to pay back?"

"Close to fifteen thousand."

His voice was calm, and only as loud as needed for me to hear over the pulsing music. But he glanced away a lot, and kept jiggling his ice, and I knew it wasn't an easy story to tell.

I fought to come up with something to say, but my brain was stuffed to the leaking point, and I didn't know what to think, much less say. "So . . . if you were gonna wait to contact us until you paid the rest of the money back, why are you telling me now?"

"Because I didn't know the truth until Junie begged me to find you."

"The truth?" I echoed, hesitant.

"That you guys were homeless, and she was in jail. She told me you had an apartment here in town."

"She actually told you that?"

"Yeah, she listed the address when she registered you for school. It's a real address. I've driven by it a number of times."

I frowned at the table as Mitzi's words came back to me. *That far? How'd you end up at this school?* "But if she didn't want you to know about us, why would she send me to the school where you worked?"

"Because she was hoping to change my mind."

I gave him a careful look. "About what?"

He sighed. "She came to Logan hoping I'd take you, Shannon. But I told her no, not until I finished paying off my debt. I think she hoped if I saw you, and got to know you at school, I'd change my mind."

My insides turned to ice, and I felt colder than I had on the boat. That's the real reason we'd come to Washington. Not because jobs paid better, but so Aunt Junie could get rid of me. She'd never wanted me. I'd been right all along. I could usually hide a lot by gritting my teeth. But not this, this was too big. I ducked my head as tears squeezed out between my lashes.

"Hey." A heavy hand settled over mine, and it startled me a little, because I couldn't ever remember a man putting his hand on mine. But there was something so solid and safe about it, something that made me want to grab on tight.

"Hey," he repeated gently. "She promised your mom she'd take care of you, Shannon, and she was making you live in a car. It's darn tough to carry a load of guilt that heavy. Can you blame her for wanting to see you someplace better?"

I swallowed, forced myself to think. I remembered Aunt Junie saying how hard it was to look at me, that I was a reminder of how she was failing Mom. At the time I didn't get it, but now I started to. "I guess not," I mumbled. A tear plopped onto the table and I rubbed my face, embarrassed. "Sorry, I'm not usually this pathetic."

He grinned. "Pathetic? Any twelve year old brave enough to spring their dog from the pound and spend three days all alone in a salvage yard in November is definitely not pathetic."

A slow smile spread across my face. Then the waitress appeared at our table and he took his hand off mine.

"All righty," she said, "hope you folks are hungry." She set our bacon cheeseburgers and fries in front of us. "Be careful, these plates are super hot. Do you want your milkshakes now, or are you saving them for dessert?"

"Sooner's always better than later when it comes to ice-cream," Officer Murphy said.

The waitress laughed. "You bet. Be right back with 'em."

I lowered my face toward the food and let the delicious smells fill my nose. I couldn't remember the last time I'd eaten in a real restaurant. I took a big bite of cheeseburger and lost myself in the salty, greasy wonderfulness.

Officer Murphy raised his top bun, squirted on mustard and rearranged his pickles, and as I watched him, I realized something incredible—he was the only relative besides Aunt Junie I'd ever known. Most kids had cousins, or knew at least one set of grandparents, but I didn't even know my own dad. Until right then, I'd never realized just how deep a canyon all that not knowing had carved inside me, and I couldn't stop studying Officer Murphy—the shape of his face, the color of his hair, the way he held his hamburger.

He glanced up and caught me staring, and his eyes crinkled at the corners again—the hazel eyes that looked so much like Mom's. "What?" he asked.

"Did you know my dad?"

Surprise flickered across his face before he shook his head. "I didn't. I knew your mom was pregnant, that's about it. But I can tell you one thing about him." He left me hanging while he wiped his mouth with a napkin. "The guy didn't deserve you."

I didn't know what I'd expected, but it wasn't that, and I couldn't keep another smile from sneaking out. "Can I tell Mitzi about you ... that you're my uncle?"

"Shoot, yeah," he said, "I hope you tell everybody."

I figured he'd say it was okay, but the pride in his voice was a gift, and the full meaning of what was happening started to sink in. I actually had an uncle. An uncle who cared what I thought about him. Who actually wanted me in his life. And I wished there was a way to take a screenshot of feelings, because if there was, I'd take one of how I felt right then and carry it with me forever. "I don't know what to call you," I said. "You've always been Officer Murphy."

His eyebrows peaked. "Well, here's an idea, how about Uncle Donovan?"

It was so simple, but so ... weird. "In front of other people, you mean? Or just when we're alone?"

He laughed. "Whenever."

"Aunt Junie will be really surprised I know."

"I warned her I was gonna tell you."

I set my longest French fry aside for Boone and stuffed two in my mouth. I thought about Aunt Junie leading him to believe we had our own apartment. She'd lied because she was too ashamed to admit the truth. How could I fault her for that? Maybe the two of us weren't so different after all. "I want us to be together again," I said. "I don't care if we have to live in the Impala."

He snorted. "Well, I care. I've got my spare bedroom rented out to a college kid right now. But believe me, if I'd had any idea my niece was living in a car, it would've been yours."

He sounded so firm. So sure. And the way he said *my niece*, like I belonged to him, filled me with wonder all over again. Maybe that's how it would feel to have a dad—a dad who loved you and made you feel safe. I took another bite of cheeseburger to keep from tearing up again. "Why do you rent out your room?"

"It's an extra $400 a month. I told you I was trying to pay off my debt as soon as I could."

I nodded. I admired him a lot for trying to fix his mistakes, but I was also pretty sure what it meant for me and Boone. "You're gonna take me back to Trina's, aren't you?"

"Miss Kinney said you liked her."

I shrugged. "Yeah … she's nice." Then my gaze fell on the French fry I'd saved for Boone and my throat got thick.

"Tell you what," he said, "How about I keep Boone for now?"

I looked up fast, more stunned that he'd read my mind than by his offer. "Really?" I breathed. "You'd really do that?"

He smiled. "Why not? I happen to like the little doggaroo."

I didn't want Boone anywhere except with me. But still, it would be way better than the shelter. "And you'd keep him until Aunt Junie gets me back again … and could I come visit him?"

"Yes to both," he said.

And for the first time in a long while I felt a measure of peace, and I let out a long shuddery breath of relief. "Thank you," I whispered. I glanced at his hand resting there on the table, and I wished so much he'd put it back on mine.

CHAPTER SEVENTEEN

I FELL ASLEEP THE second my head hit the pillow that night at Trina's, but I woke before dawn stressing over Mitzi. I couldn't wait to tell her Officer Murphy was actually ... *my uncle*. But for that to make sense, I had to tell her the whole story, and I knew there was a good chance she'd run the other way. And I so, so didn't want her to do that.

"I'm sorry I told Officer Murphy about the fork lift," Mitzi gushed, as soon as we were finally alone at lunch. "I was just really freaked out for you."

Her sudden outburst caught me off guard, because I'd expected to be the one having to defend myself. But her hands were twisted into a pretzel, and her eyes were so big and earnest I almost laughed. "It's okay," I said, with as much grace as I could manage. "I'm not mad. I probably would've done the same thing."

She beamed. "Woo-hoo! I was afraid you'd never talk to me again. So will you finally tell me why you ran away?"

My toes curled inside my shoes. I'd rehearsed what to say a hundred times, but nothing I'd planned seemed good enough. I scooted green beans around my lunch tray. "Remember when you asked where I lived, and I told you over by the Flying J?"

Her forehead wrinkled. "Yeah?"

"Well, it wasn't near the truck stop, it *was* the truck stop. My Aunt Junie and I were living in our car. We've been homeless for almost two months."

Mitzi eyed me intently, her mouth quivering into a half smile, like I'd told a joke and she was waiting for the punchline. "You're kidding me, right?"

My breath locked tight in my stomach. "Nope."

A blush travelled up her face. "No?"

"It's only temporary," I quickly added. "As soon as Aunt Junie gets a job we'll have our own place again."

"But that picture on your phone…"

"That was our house in Plummer, where we lived before we came here."

"Oh," she said, softly.

I watched a kid pour chocolate milk on his mashed potatoes and waited for Mitzi to pass sentence on me. I wondered if that's how Aunt Junie felt when she met with the judge.

She focused on her lunch tray for a long minute, then she glanced up and wiggled her eyebrows in that silly way

174

only Mitzi could. "So, um ... I guess I can't come to your house, but you could still come to mine."

My relief exploded in a goofy snort. She had no idea how incredible she was, and I knew I'd never be able to explain it to her. I reached over and gave her a one armed hug.

"Okaaaay," she pulled away, laughing. "Not in front of everybody, you weirdo. But you still haven't told me why you ran away."

"I was getting to it," I said, "but the short version is I had to rescue my dog."

She glanced at her phone. "Spill fast," she said. "We've only got ten minutes and I wanna hear everything."

The details I didn't have time for right then, I filled in later that evening when we talked on the phone for another hour. She begged me to come over and spend Saturday night, but Miss Kinney said she couldn't allow it since she didn't know Mitzi or her family. But then Uncle Donovan talked with her, and the no miraculously turned into a yes. He even offered to drive me to Mitzi's himself, and I realized there could be some real advantages to having a cop in the family.

Uncle Donovan picked me up from Trina's Saturday morning at nine thirty. I climbed into his Jeep, thankful Megan had let me borrow clean jeans and a T-shirt while my other clothes were getting washed. "How's Boone?" I asked. "Has he been okay for you?"

"Yep. He spends most of his time on the back of my sofa looking out the window."

I felt a sharp pang. "He's probably looking for me."

"Want to visit him?"

I hesitated. Every part of me ached to say yes, but I shook my head. "It'd be too hard to walk in and have to leave him again a few minutes later."

"Makes sense. We'll figure out a time when you can come stay awhile."

"Okay. Thanks for talking Miss Kinney into letting me go to Mitzi's."

"You're welcome." He flashed me a mysterious smile. "You mind making a quick stop first?"

"You're the boss."

"I just thought maybe you'd like to see Junie."

"Really!"

"Yeah, they moved her to the rehab clinic last evening. I told her I'd bring you by."

"I thought she had one more day in jail."

"Technically she did, but the staff tries to avoid weekend admissions if they can."

I puffed out a soft breath as my stomach filled with crickets. The last time I'd seen Aunt Junie had been at the police station, and the last time we'd talked, I'd said those mean things. I wondered if she'd want to see me.

Saint Joseph's Hospital sprawled over two city blocks, but the rehab clinic was a much smaller building in back. I nervously followed Uncle Donovan up to the main desk in the lobby, and a friendly woman directed us down the tiled hall to an open area called the commons. Aunt Junie waited on a paisley couch by a big window overlooking the parking lot, and I knew she was watching for us.

"Hi," I called, and she whirled around.

"Oh ... you," she cried, hurrying over and grabbing my shoulders. "Jeez, Shannon. I don't know if I should hug you or holler at you." Then she threw her arms around me.

"I'm sorry for scaring you," I said. "But I had to rescue Boone."

She pulled back and looked me in the face. Her olive green jumpsuit gave her a washed out look, but her eyes were clear, and her hair was brushed and pulled back from her face. She gave Uncle Donovan a quick once-over before fixing her gaze back on me. "So," she said, "I see you met your uncle."

"Um ... yeah," I said. And then I forced a giggle, because I didn't trust myself to say anything else right then. I wanted to ask how she and Mom could have lied to me all those years. Why they ever thought it was okay to keep something so important a secret. But now wasn't the time.

"I know," she said, reading my mind. "I've got a whole lot of explaining to do. Just don't hate me, okay?"

I smiled. "You look good, Aunt Junie. You really do."

177

She puffed out her cheeks. "I've been sober for seven days now."

"Congratulations," I said, not sure if that was the right response.

Uncle Donovan nodded. "Good job," he said.

She bit her lip and turned toward him, as if she knew she couldn't pretend he was invisible forever. She gave him an awkward hug. "Thank you, Donny. For finding Shannon, and for . . . not turning your back on us."

He gave her a couple thumps on the back. "I'm not a turn my back kind of guy," he said.

Aunt Junie stepped away and grabbed my hand. "Come on and sit down over here."

We sat on the couch by the window and Aunt Junie asked about Trina, school and Boone, and what had happened in the salvage yard. Then she told us about the team of counselors she'd met that morning, and how her rehab classes were supposed to help. Way too soon a brown haired man came and told Aunt Junie it was time for a therapy session. I wanted to tell him to go away, that we needed more time. But Aunt Junie popped right up like it was something important, and I knew it probably was.

She walked us out to the main entrance and gave me another hug. "I'm gonna get us back together soon, bug. I promise."

"Okay," I whispered in her ear. "And I'm sorry about that stuff I said to you on the phone." Then I quickly pulled away and trailed Uncle Donovan back out to the Jeep, feeling strangely unsettled. I buckled my seat belt and cracked my knuckles.

He glanced over at me with raised eyebrows. "She's looking pretty good, don't you think?"

"Yep," I said, because it seemed like an honest answer. But the full truth was, I didn't want to drive away and leave Aunt Junie behind. I wanted us back together. I wanted Boone. I wanted a home. But wanting didn't get you any further than a car without an engine, and the helpless feeling was like ten gallons of liquid impatience sloshing around inside me, just waiting for a chance to explode through my skin. I cracked my knuckles again.

Mitzi lived in a perfectly average yellow house across from a 7-Eleven convenience store, and the fact that it wasn't some big, fancy place I could never dream of living made me feel a little better. Mitzi met us at the door and introduced us to her mother. Mrs. Adams had a long face, salt and pepper hair clamped in a messy bun, and bright blue ballerina slippers.

She laughed when she caught me staring at them. "Excuse the way I look, but if I don't have to go anywhere, I lounge."

Mitzi gawked at Uncle Donovan. "You look so different without your uniform," she said, then she put a hand over her mouth to cover her giggles.

He nodded. "Yeah, I get that a lot. But I'm still the same guy so you better behave."

"I just made peach coffee cake," Mrs. Adams said, gesturing toward the kitchen. "Can I get you both a piece?"

"Sounds too good to pass up," Uncle Donovan said, and we all traipsed into the kitchen. Mitzi swept the table clear of a laptop and a bunch of real estate brochures, and Mrs. Adams set out four plates. Mitzi wolfed down her coffee cake and tapped her fingernails on the table while I finished mine. Then she grabbed my arm and towed me down the hall to her bedroom.

I waved a quick goodbye to Uncle Donovan, and he winked at me. "Have fun. Either Miss Kinney or I will pick you up tomorrow."

Mitzi flung open her bedroom door. "Look, I cleaned it up just for you. You should feel honored."

"Gee, thanks," I said, glancing around the room. "You shouldn't have." She had vintage dolls on a shelf above her bed and a whole bookshelf full of DVD's. I walked over and fingered the set of Sephora lip gloss on her dresser—Aunt Junie's favorite brand of makeup. I checked the labels to see if she had Pink Teaser. "So what are we gonna do?"

She waved her phone in front of me. "Do you like the comedy clips on YouTube? I've got some great Daniel Tosh."

"Sure," I said, though I'd never heard of him, and I couldn't remember the last time I'd gotten a chance to watch YouTube.

We spent the next hour settled back against her Snoopy body pillow, our heads nearly touching, giggling over Daniel Tosh's impersonations of the president, and his jokes about public bathrooms and the winter Olympics. For the first time in ages things felt magically normal, and I was determined not to take a second of it for granted.

My phone vibrated against my hip, and I pulled it out, thinking it might be Aunt Junie. I didn't recognize the number. "Probably spam," I said.

Mitzi giggled. "Maybe you've been specially selected for a cruise to the Bahamas. My dad gets those all the time."

I smirked. "Hey, if it is, let's go .... Hello?"

"Yes, good afternoon," said a woman's voice. "I'm trying to reach Shannon O'Reilly."

I propped myself up on an elbow. "This is Shannon."

"Oh, very good. My name is Marjorie Silver. I'm with the Silver Heart Academy of Cosmetology."

CHAPTER EIGHTEEN

I NEARLY DROPPED THE phone. "Oh! Oooooh."

Mitzi paused the video and fixed me with a curious look.

The woman laughed. "It seems as though you recognize my name."

"Um ... yeah," I said. "I sent you the essay."

"You did. And I love your essay. It's beautiful."

"No way." The words popped out before I could stop them.

"It's one of the most heartfelt essays I've ever read. And I'd be honored to consider your aunt for one of our silver heart awards."

I braced myself to keep from toppling off Mitzi's bed. "To c-consider her?" I stammered.

"Yes. I always meet with the applicants and get to know them a bit before making a final decision. But your aunt is certainly a strong contender. Might she have any time available tomorrow?"

I opened my mouth, but no sound came out. I threw Mitzi a desperate look, not sure if I should laugh or cry. What in the world was I supposed to say? How did I even begin to explain what was going on in our lives right then? "Um ... could you hang on just a minute?"

"Of course," Mrs. Silver said. "Did I catch you at a bad time? I can call back later if it's more convenient."

"No, no it's fine. Could you just please ... hold on?"

"What's going on?" Mitzi whispered. "What essay?"

I put a finger to my lips and shoved the phone under the Snoopy pillow. My heart felt like it might pound into pieces. "It's part of the story I didn't tell you," I whispered. "I entered a contest to try and help my aunt go back to cosmetology school like she's always wanted to."

Mitzi bounced onto her knees and clasped her hands. "And you won? Cool! Waaaaay cool."

"It's not for sure yet," I said. "The lady from the school wants to meet with her first."

"Well ... that's good, right?"

I grabbed my face. "Yes. I mean ... No! I can't tell her Aunt Junie's in rehab. What am I supposed to say?"

Mitzi stopped bouncing. "Ooooh." She bit her lip and gazed up at her light fixture. "Yeah, okay ... "

I stared at her as the seconds ticked past. I knew it wasn't fair to make her figure out what to do. I'm the one who'd written the essay. "Mitzi," I said, "I know this is gonna sound like a really weird question, but is your mom as nice as she seems?"

Mitzi pulled back, like she sensed a trap. "Um ... most of the time."

"Think she might be willing to give me a ride to the hospital tomorrow?"

"Maybe. I mean ... probably."

"Good enough." I cleared my throat and grabbed the phone. "Um, Mrs. Silver? I'm really sorry for making you wait, and I'm really excited for you to meet my aunt. Tomorrow would be good."

Mitzi squealed. I cut her a sharp look, and she slapped a hand over her mouth.

"I'm so glad," Mrs. Silver said. "And I'm excited to meet both of you. I'll need directions to your home."

I suddenly felt woozy. Directions to my home? *Gee ... I'm sorry. I don't have one of those right now.* I cleared my throat again. "It's ... it's a little hard to find. How about if we meet at Saint Joseph's. Do you know where that is?"

"The hospital? Yes, of course."

"Okay, good. Let's meet in the back parking lot, where it's not so busy, and then you can follow us from there."

There were several heartbeats of silence before Mrs. Silver laughed. "Well, all right, dear, if that's what you'd like to do. The back parking lot of Saint Joseph's. I'll be in a red Mercury. What type of car should I watch for?"

"Your car is red," I repeated, waving my hand in an urgent circle in Mitzi's face. "Okay, we'll be driving a ... "

"White," Mitzi mouthed. "Four doors."

"A white four door. I'll watch for you."

"All right. How about ten o'clock?"

"Perfect."

"Wonderful, Shannon. Then it's a date. I'll see you in the morning."

"Okay," I managed. "Thank you." My muscles felt like spaghetti noodles and I slumped back against the pillow.

Mitzi gave a hoot. "Want me to get Mom?"

I swallowed. "Not really," I said, "but I guess you better."

Mrs. Adams waltzed into the bedroom with a trusting smile. She perched on the edge of the bed with her hands draped over her knees, and I felt bad for what I was about to dump on her. She didn't even know me. She'd think I was crazy. Her face paled as she listened, then she shook her head in disbelief, eventually she started to laugh.

Long after Mrs. Adams had gone to bed, Mitzi and I stayed awake, plotting in excited whispers. But once Mitzi drifted off, doubt swooped in on me like a huge, dark bird, whispering that if Mrs. Silver discovered the ugly truth about Aunt Junie, she'd decide she didn't deserve to win. And I wanted her to win, hungered for it with every ounce of my being. Not just because I wanted to prove how smart and resourceful I was, but because I wanted to make something good happen for Aunt Junie. I understood her better now, understood some of the choices she'd made and how much she'd sacrificed for me. And what better way to repay her than to help her believe in herself again? But Mrs. Silver didn't know all that. What if I couldn't make her understand?

I chased the scary doubts away by thinking about Uncle Donovan, how hard it must have been for him to admit his mistakes, not only to me, but to the people he cheated. And how brave Megan had been to tell the school counselor about the shameful stuff happening in her family. If they could do it, I could too. I listened to Mitzi's soft breathing beside me and remembered how I'd trusted her with the truth and she hadn't run away. Maybe Mrs. Silver wouldn't either. And a sense of peace finally let me sleep.

By the time Mrs. Adams drove us to Saint Joseph's the next morning, the dark, scary bird of doubt was back, and my stomach was queasy. I sat in the back seat with Mitzi, my chilled hands locked around each other. "Are you sure you guys won't come in?" I asked. "I really want you to."

Mrs. Adams nodded. "I know, sweetie. But I really feel like this is a family thing. Your aunt doesn't even know us. She might be really embarrassed to have us stick our noses in her business."

"But what should I say to Mrs. Silver? She just thinks she's gonna follow me home."

Mrs. Adams met my eyes in the rearview mirror. "Tell her you have something you need to share with her, Shannon. Just level with her."

I nodded. It was what I'd already decided to do ... if I didn't hyperventilate in the meantime. "Can you at least get out and meet her?"

"Of course." Mrs. Adams said. "But you'll see, everything will work out."

"That's her," Mitzi said, pointing, as we pulled into the hospital parking lot. "It's a red Mercury."

I clutched her hand. "I think I'm gonna pass out."

She giggled. "As long as you don't hurl."

We pulled up alongside the red car, and Mrs. Adams shut off the engine. She turned to look at me. "Okay. Ready ... set ... go!"

We all climbed out together, and Mrs. Silver got out as well. She was one of the prettiest old ladies I'd ever seen, with hair the same color as her name, her makeup soft and perfectly blended. I didn't think I could picture a more perfect example of a beauty school owner.

I tried to say hello, and ended up coughing instead. My cheeks burned. "Hi," I began again. "I'm Shannon."

"And I'm Marjorie Silver." She took my hand in both of hers. "I'm so pleased to meet you." She nodded to Mrs. Adams with a twinkle in her eye. "Might you perhaps be her aunt?"

"Oh, heavens no," she said, laughing. "I'm just a friend, Sarah Adams, and this is my daughter, Mitzi. The girls spent last night together so I volunteered to chauffeur."

"I see," Mrs. Silver said. "That was very kind of you." She looked at me. "Well, now, is your aunt waiting for us?"

Mrs. Adams gave me a reassuring wink. I took a soft breath. "Yeah," I said, "she is waiting for us. But she's not home. She's here."

"Here? At the hospital?"

"You know what?" Mrs. Adams said, before I could explain. "How about if Mitzi and I take a quick walk around the block? We'll give you two a chance to talk for a few minutes." She gave Mitzi a sharp nod.

Mitzi's face fell. "Oh. Oh … yeah, sure."

I waited, hoping I didn't pass out in front of Mrs. Silver as Mitzi and her mom hurried across the parking lot. Then I raised my chin and met Mrs. Silver's puzzled eyes. "I know this will probably change everything," I said in a rush, "and I totally understand if it does. But I didn't tell you everything about my aunt in the essay. She's here at Saint Joseph's because she's in rehab. I know I should've told you before, but I thought … I mean, I didn't know how you'd feel about …" The breath I'd started with was gone, and my voice fizzled.

Mrs. Silver waited patiently, as if she wanted to make sure I'd finished. Then she put a hand on my shoulder. "I can appreciate how that's a difficult thing to tell a stranger. Did you think it might disqualify your aunt from consideration?"

I nodded. "The rules said the awards were for people who couldn't go to school because of … or due to … " I struggled to remember the exact wording.

"Due to problems beyond their control," Mrs. Sliver finished for me. She was silent for a long moment. "That's true," she said. "It could be said that some addictions are a person's own fault. But I believe others are more like a disease, out of a person's control."

"She didn't have much of a drinking problem until my Mom died. But she still took care of me," I added. "She always has."

"This rehab program she's enrolled in, was it her idea?"

I lowered my eyes. "No. A judge told her she had to. But she understands … now. She wants to get better."

Mrs. Sliver glanced toward the building. "I'm guessing she's expecting you this morning, but not me. Am I right?"

I gave her a sheepish smile. "Actually, she's not expecting me either."

Her eyes widened before she shook her head and laughed. "Oh, dear. Well, you know what they say, nothing ventured nothing gained. Let's go meet her and see what happens, shall we?"

A grin slipped across my face, and I felt light enough to skate on air. "Good idea," I said.

Aunt Junie sat at a table in the commons, wearing the same green jumpsuit, her head bent over the paperwork in front of her. "There she is," I whispered.

"Go ahead," Mrs. Silver said. "I'll wait a moment."

I took a soft breath as I headed for the table. "Hi, Aunt Junie."

Her head popped up. "Shannon? What in the world?" She jumped up and gave me a hug. "Where's your uncle?"

"He's not with me," I said. "I have a surprise for you, okay? Someone else I want you to meet." I gestured to Mrs. Silver.

Aunt Junie smoothed a hand over her hair and watched nervously as she approached. "Hi. You must be Trina?"

Mrs. Silver raised her eyebrows.

"No," I said. "Aunt Junie, this is Mrs. Silver. She's … uh, she's … " I hesitated. How exactly was I supposed to introduce her?

"I'm from the Silver Heart Academy of Cosmetology," she said, holding out a hand to Aunt Junie. "It's a pleasure to meet you."

Aunt Junie's mouth fell open. "The Silver Heart Academy of … " her voice squeaked to nothing and made me giggle.

"I know I've caught you completely off guard," Mrs. Silver said. "I hope you can forgive me for bursting in this way."

"Come on," I said. "Let's go sit, and I'll tell you the whole story."

I led the way over to the couch by the window where we'd sat on our first visit. I let Aunt Junie and Mrs. Silver have the couch, and I rolled up a chair and sat across from them. It was more fun that way because I got to watch all of Aunt Junie's crazy expressions as I confessed to researching the school, writing the essay and finally getting the call from Mrs. Silver. Then I sat back and let Mrs. Silver explain how she and her husband first thought up the essay award and how touched she was by what I'd written. She reached into her bright green handbag and removed a sheet of paper. "May I share your essay, Shannon?"

My heart flipped. I didn't want to hear it read aloud. It was way too personal. "If you want," I said, jumping up. "I'll get us some water."

I scurried over to the bottled water dispenser at the far end of the room. I took my time filling three paper cups while I watched Aunt Junie out of the corner of my eye. And when I saw her slowly bow her head and cover her face with her hands, my eyes filled with tears.

I carried over the water and carefully placed the cups on the coffee table near the couch. Aunt Junie motioned to me, and I sat down beside her. She lifted her hands and let them drop in her lap. "Oh, bug. I don't even know what to say. This is just ... insanely crazy. I don't deserve you."

I gripped the couch cushion to keep from floating up to the ceiling. "Why not?" I said. "Think about all the stuff you did for Mom and me."

Mrs. Silver sat quietly, waiting until Aunt Junie finally sat back. Then she smiled and checked her watch. "There's no need for me to take up any more of your day, and I'm sure you need time to digest all this information we've dumped on you. But I want you to know, if you can arrange your schedule, we'd be honored to have you attend the Silver Heart Academy." She pulled two business cards from her purse and handed one to each of us. "Here's how you can reach me once you've had a chance to think it over."

Aunt Junie took the card with a laugh. "What's to think over? I'd looooove to attend your school. It would be amazing. But I have another couple of weeks here, and then I need to find Shannon and me a place to live, and . . . "

"Don't feel rushed," Mrs. Silver said. "Take whatever time you need. We offer two courses per year. One begins in April, and another in October."

"April?" I said. "That would give us time to get stuff settled, Aunt Junie. You'd be ready by spring, don't you think?"

She took a deep breath and let it out slowly. "Maybe so," she said. "Maybe so."

Mrs. Silver patted her hand. "Like I said, take your time, and contact me when you feel ready." She stood and winked at me. "Don't forget, Shannon, you have friends outside."

I sucked in a breath. "Oh, my gosh," I said, laughing. "I forgot all about them."

"Forgot who?" Aunt Junie asked.

"My friend Mitzi and her mom," I said. "They brought me here. I gotta go."

Aunt Junie jumped up. "Wait, I'll walk you out. I wanna meet them."

I never saw Mrs. Silver leave. Mitzi dragged me over to a gravelly island in the parking lot, and by the time I got through answering her questions, the red Mercury was gone. The airy sound of Aunt Junie's voice caught my attention, and I watched her smiling and gesturing to Mrs. Adams. I couldn't remember the last time I'd heard her sound genuinely happy. And I knew I'd done more than just give a gift to Aunt Junie, I'd given both of us the gift of a new chance. And I was so glad I'd gambled on the essay, that I'd trusted Mrs. Silver with the truth. Maybe my teacher was right after all. If you had enough will, maybe sometimes there really *was* a way.

CHAPTER NINETEEN

O N THE TWO MONTH anniversary of Aunt Junie's sobriety, Uncle Donovan took us out to celebrate. Mitzi came too. We started with pizza at home, all four of us scrunched around Uncle Donovan's little kitchen table, Boone happily snapping up the bits of sausage I dropped him. After dinner we got hot fudge sundaes at Baskin-N-Robbin's before going to the Metro arena to see a Disney on Ice performance of Frozen.

Mitzi and I sat beside each other in the chilly stadium, my Seattle Seahawks blanket tucked over our laps. Mitzi twisted like a worm, watching for any signs the show was about to start. But I was just happy to be there, to feel like I fit in with all the other people around us.

Aunt Junie sat on my other side, touching up her lip-stick. She rubbed her lips together to blend the color and then turned to me. "Is it even? I lost my mirror somewhere in that mess of a bedroom."

"It's perfect," I said. "It even matches your plum shirt."

"Really?" She winked. "You'd almost think I planned it that way."

"You look really good, Aunt Junie. Are you feeling okay?"

"I'm fine, bug. How many times have I told you not to worry about me?"

I shrugged. "I'm not," I said, but it wasn't true. Even though she hadn't had a drink for sixty days, our new life still felt as delicate and fragile as a china cup. I'd feel better once she'd made it past the three month mark, what her therapist called "the danger zone" for relapse. It was one of the many tidbits I'd learned during the Power Point presentation the staff showed us on Aunt Junie's last day at Saint Joseph's. After the slide show, there been a nail biting two hour meeting between Uncle Donovan, Miss Kinney, Aunt Junie and two of her counselors.

I spent the meeting with my mouth shut and my stomach cramped, listening to the adults debate the best thing for Aunt Junie and me. The only thing everyone *did* agree on was that finishing rehab, finding a new place to live, trying to find work, and starting cosmetology school all within a few months would put too much pressure on Aunt Junie—a recipe for relapse. It was Uncle Donovan who finally came up with a solution everyone could live with.

He helped his student renter find a new place to live so Aunt Junie and I could have the spare room. She'd gotten hired as a cashier at Rosauers not long after. Half of each paycheck went to Uncle Donovan, and the other half went into savings. Starting in April, Aunt Junie would attend the Silver Heart Academy in the evenings, and then after she graduated, Mitzi's mom promised to help us find an affordable apartment of our own.

It wasn't a perfect situation—Aunt Junie, Boone and me had to share a bed in a too-small room. Uncle Donovan hogged the TV remote, and he and Aunt Junie butted heads... a lot. But it was all okay, because that kind of thing didn't seem like a big deal compared to the way things had been before.

The stadium lights suddenly dimmed and Mitzi grabbed my arm. "Woo-hoo, it's finally time."

I squinted against the bright spotlights as all the characters glided out onto the ice in their dazzling costumes. "Who's your favorite?" Mitzi asked.

"Olaf," I said, pointing to the adorable snowman who looked like he was struggling to stay upright. "How about you?"

"Kristoff, of course," she said, "he's hot."

Uncle Donovan raised an eyebrow and Mitzi and I both dissolved into giggles. Then the orchestra music got too loud for talking, and I settled back under the blanket and lost myself in the show. I liked the movie the first time

I'd seen it, but I hadn't really paid much attention to the actual story of a town trapped in eternal winter. But as I watched it now, I couldn't help relating to it in a whole new way. And by the time the kingdom of Arendelle emerged into a bright new spring, I felt just as hopeful as Anna and Elsa. Because I felt like I was emerging too, from a really dark time, to something much better.

It was clear and crisp by the time the show ended and we made our way across the dimly lit parking area to the far lot. Mitzi and I trotted ahead of Aunt Junie and Uncle Donovan, giggling and arguing over the best parts of the show. We reached the Jeep and were waiting for Uncle Donovan to unlock it, when a small red glow caught my eye. I peered closer to see a man propped against the base of the overpass leading into the arena, the tip of his cigarette glowing.

Mitzi sucked in a breath and quickly looked around, as if she wanted to make sure we weren't alone. But for some reason, I didn't feel afraid. The man wore tan work boots, exactly like the ones Mr. Henry the construction worker had worn when he visited our class. "Hi," I said, hesitantly. "Do you build houses?"

The man scratched beneath his stocking hat as he took another drag on his cigarette. "When there's work," he said, his voice gravelly.

Mitzi grabbed my elbow. "What are you doing?" she whispered.

I wasn't sure how to answer that, because I really didn't know what I was doing. It just seemed important to let the man know I'd seen him, that he wasn't invisible. I shook free of her hand and stepped forward. "Did you know that the Methodist Church on Brown Street serves free breakfast every Thursday?"

He snorted, and I caught a flash of white teeth. "That right?"

"Yeah," I said. "The blueberry pancakes are awesome."

"You tried 'em?"

"Yeah," I said, and for once I didn't feel ashamed. "I ate there not long ago."

I heard the "click" of the Jeep unlocking and knew Uncle Donovan was behind me. But I stayed still, mesmerized by the on and off glow of the man's cigarette. I'm not sure what held me there, but I did know one thing—I'd never think of homelessness in quite the same way again.

Uncle Donovan cleared his throat. "C'mon, Shannon," he said, kindly. "Time to head home."

And I thought about that word *home*, how much those four little letters stood for, and how glad I was that Aunt Junie and I had found the path back. I suddenly bounded across to the man and thrust out my Seattle Seahawks blanket. "Here," I said. "It's really warm."

The man shifted his gaze past me to Uncle Donovan, as if he expected him to say no. But then he reached out and took it.

I hopped back to the Jeep before I heard the gravelly voice again. "Hey, kid?" he said. "God bless."

"You too," I said, glancing back over my shoulder. And I smiled to myself as I climbed in.

ABOUT THE AUTHOR

Dianna Dorisi Winget has been writing since she was nine years old, when she would stuff notebooks under her bed to keep prying eyes from seeing her masterpieces. Today she's a little less shy about sharing her work. Dianna lives in the mountains of north Idaho with her husband and a bossy Daschund—one of many dogs she's adopted over the years from local animal shelters. She loves to hear from and respond to young readers. Find out more about Dianna and connect with her on social media.

WEBSITE:
http://diannawinget.com

GOODREADS:
http://www.goodreads.com/author/show/5573825.
Dianna_Dorisi_Winget

TWITTER:
https://Twitter.com/DiannaMWinget

INSTAGRAM:
https://www.instagram.com/dianna.writes/